THE PUSH-BUTTON SPY

. Also by Leigh James .
THE CHAMELEON FILE
THE CAPITOL HILL AFFAIR

The Push-Button Spy

BY LEIGH JAMES

PRENTICE-HALL, INC.
ENGLEWOOD CLIFFS, N. J.

THE PUSH-BUTTON SPY

.PROLOGUE.

The Wiener Waltzer Express, twenty minutes out of Innsbruck and a half hour behind schedule, moved rapidly westward through heavy mist and rain toward the Swiss frontier. A door on one of the first-class carriages abruptly swung open and a man's figure dropped limply downward onto the graveled embankment beside the westbound track. Stirring a small dust cloud among the stones at the point of impact, it violently rolled down the embankment at an angle that followed the momentum of the train, its arms and legs whipping out grotesquely from the body, until it came to rest in a muddy ditch which divided the railroad right-of-way from the surrounding fields. It lay spread-eagled and face down in a small puddle of water as the train disappeared into the mist, the carriage door hanging open, buffeted back and forth on its hinges by the wet streams of air that swirled about it.

A farmer discovered the body an hour later. In four more hours, after an exchange of wires between the local Austrian police, Interpol at Paris, and the American Embassies at Vienna and Bucharest, the news reached the gray concrete redoubt of CIA headquarters hidden behind the palisades of the Potomac River a few miles upstream from Washington.

The Man Behind the Desk in a modest office suite on one of the upper floors was lighting his pipe with a wooden kitchen match as his visitor entered. "This is a hot one, Ernie," he said between puffs, motioning the saturnine man in the rumpled putty-colored raincoat into a chair. He blew out the match and drew on his pipe contentedly for a moment. "You know Fenwick?"

"Slightly. We walk a different beat."

"He was murdered in the Tyrol on an international express a few hours ago."

Sessena carefully unwrapped a piece of chewing gum and pushed it into his mouth. "Where was he going?"

The Man Behind the Desk nodded. "That's it. He was posted to the Embassy at Bucharest. We didn't know that he was on the move."

"He has a reputation of being one of the good ones. Was he on to anything?"

The Man Behind the Desk tapped on a file before him with the stem of his pipe. "He may have been. He was sent to Bucharest three years ago to monitor the Balkans. Romania doesn't follow the Soviet foreign policy line these days with the slavish devotion of the other satellites, particularly where anti-Jewish policy is concerned. As a result, there is a little more room for our boys to maneuver than there is in the other Communist capitals of Eastern Europe. Since the 1967 Six-Day War between Israel and the Arabs, Bucharest has become a city where the Arabs and the Israelis wheel and deal in foreign intelligence. Fenwick grew up with the market so to speak. Within the last year, particularly, he became an important source of middle eastern intelligence for us. However, Bucharest is still a provincial capital compared with Vienna where espionage and intelligence are concerned, so we kept a string on Fenwick through Bob Scott in Vienna. Fenwick made periodic trips to Vienna to report to Scott."

"And this wasn't one of them?"

The Man Behind the Desk slowly shook his head. "Fenwick usually flew to Vienna. His trips were planned ahead. As a courtesy, he notified the Ambassador in Bucharest when he left the country. This time he took the train. He informed no one of the trip. He bypassed Vienna and was heading west, probably to Zürich, possibly to Paris."

"And the opposition took him out."

"It looks like it, Ernesto mio. It sure looks like it."

Sessena lit a cigarette and waited.

"I want you to drop in over there, Ernie. Fenwick was a bachelor and had no family. Visit this little village," he looked at a cable on his desk, "Zirl is the name of the place, and claim the body as the next of kin. You are in a way."

"Sister?"

The Man Behind the Desk didn't smile. "Let's say a cousin. You can then travel under your own name." The pipe was out and he relit it. "Scott will accompany you from Vienna, representing the Embassy, sorry a fellow American got it, nasty business, that sort of thing. Nose around, talk things over with Scott. Decide where we go from here. Do we restaff Bucharest? What does this do to our Balkan operation? Can we get a line on the bastards that did it? What don't we know that we ought to know?"

Sessena nodded.

"Miss Hare has arranged your flight to Vienna. Scott will meet your plane. Play it by ear. No messages to me via code or otherwise. I'll hear it all verbally when you get back."

Sessena got up from his chair and pushed out his cigarette in an ashtray on the desk.

"And, by the way, Ernie, in Fenwick's last reports he passed on a report that Israel was developing an A-bomb capability and experimenting with nerve gas. We're checking it out elsewhere. It may be an Arab plant, but bear it in mind anyway."

Sessena looked at him somberly for a moment. "I was waiting for the twister on this."

The Man Behind the Desk laughed shortly. "What in hell do you care? You aren't running for public office."

"No. I'm just running. See you around." He picked up his air tickets, travelers checks, and passport from Miss Hare in the outside office. Her aquiline Negro face softened in a fleeting smile. "Good luck."

"Thanks, chick."

.4.

In the cold, impersonal building passageway he lit a cigarette, hunched his shoulders in his soiled raincoat and rang for the elevator. While waiting, he sneezed and wondered if he was getting a cold.

.1.

The setting sun's rays fingered the jet as it circled low over the Wienerwald and the Danube, obeying the landing instructions from the control tower at Vienna airport. The reflection off its aluminum skin turned it for a brief moment into a mirror filled with a golden light before it passed into the late afternoon shadows and glided gracefully to the ground.

Robert Scott stood on the air terminal's observation deck, his camel's hair coat collar turned up against the raw wind of late March, and watched the airplane move rapidly down the runway, the roar of its engines in reverse thrust rolling across a half mile of distance to shake the windows behind him. As it turned around at the end of the runway, its multiple lights flashing red in the approaching dusk, he reentered the air terminal building and walked leisurely toward the customs area through which international passengers deplaned.

At six-feet-three, wiry and slim, he towered above the stolid crowd waiting for the arrival of the passengers from the West. With a thatch of unruly blond hair that had just missed being red, and a wide humorous mouth, he was unmistakably American. Already, in his late twenties, there were faint lines about his mouth and eyes that indicated the flood and ebb of his ready grin. People liked him. He seemed always poised to go out and meet life, to savor and enjoy it. He generated a human warmth. Once he had smiled at them they were unaware that he was not handsome. Only the very perceptive noticed the unsmiling intensity of his blue eyes or the way his lips could purse into a thin line when he was concentrating.

He lit a cigarette and over his cupped hands shielding the flame of the match caught a glimpse of the stocky figure of Ernie Sessena through the door leading into the customs area. The door had been propped open by a uniformed customs official and passengers were beginning to file through it, some trudging off alone, others greeted by boisterous friends and relatives.

Sessena stood patiently, waiting for a customs official to complete a cursory inspection of the contents of his single scuffed leather case. The official nodded peremptorily at Sessena, marked a scrawled letter on the case with a piece of white chalk, and moved down the low counter to the luggage of another passenger.

As Sessena emerged through the open door, free at last from the official entry procedures, Scott extended one hand for the case and slapped the older man on the shoulder with the other. "Hiya, Ernie?"

"Not bad, Scottie. I got leg cramps and a bellyache, but that's par for a transatlantic flight."

"I've got a car in the parking lot. Come this way."

Scott swung the case into the trunk of a small black Opel sedan. "Hell of a thing about Fenwick."

"Yes. Pretty rough." Sessena then remained silent until they had left the airport and were on the highway leading to Vienna. His grim profile was faintly outlined by the instrument panel lights and the fading remnants of daylight. "Any leads here?"

"Not yet. I didn't even know Fenwick was in Austria. Apparently I've got a lot to catch up on."

"You think he was leading a double life?"

"It's possible. He was a good agent and as a good agent I gave him a lot of discretion. He could have worked on a number of things on the side if he had been that kind of a fool."

"He wouldn't have been the first."

"No, nor the last."

Sessena looked out of the streaked window at the sodden landscape. "I thought this was 'The Land of Smiles.'"

"That was some time ago." Scott downshifted as the Opel went up a curving grade. Traffic increased as they entered the city, leaving the highway to roll down cobbled streets between gray stone buildings that stretched in rows like parallel walls reaching to an indefinite horizon. The ornate facades of equal height were broken from time to time by domes atop circular corner demi-towers, chimneys belching the last brown breath of winter's smoke, and occasional mansard roofs upon which lay soiled white traces of a late season snow. Tall, high-arching street lights shone dimly in an evening mist that was rising from the Danube as the temperature fell to flow softly and ubiquitously through the curving narrow streets of the medieval inner city. An occasional neon sign in red or blue fluttered in windows or above store fronts proclaiming *Kindermoden* or *Parfumeur,* spilling its light over the narrow sidewalks and curbing and casting the remainder of the street into a contrasting and deeper darkness.

Scott swung the Opel off Ringstrasse into the outer service street and pulled up before the dimly lit entrance of the Bristol Hotel. A doorman, smelling of damp wool, opened the curbside door with a cheery, *"guten abend."*

"I'll wait in the bar while you check in," Scott said. "Then we can have some dinner."

"Just what I need." Sessena grimaced. "Let's find a health food bar."

"The place I have in mind is Hungarian."

"Good God!"

"The paprika will settle your stomach."

"Too bad you didn't get it instead of Fenwick. You're a damn sadist."

"No, I'm just hungry," Scott said cheerfully. "But don't worry. Only the good die young."

"It's too late for me and I doubt that you're eligible." Sessena followed the porter into the hotel.

Scott walked through the small, overfurnished lobby with its heavy Germanic chairs upholstered in a thick brocade of dull reds and golds and into the small barroom. He sat down at a table in the corner and ordered a scotch and soda. He was smoking his second cigarette and wondering what in hell was keeping Sessena, when a woman of about thirty-five with a full figure and light brown hair worn in a short bob entered the barroom and after a brief glance in his direction from wide-set gray eyes, sat down two tables away from him. He sensed that she was studying him furtively, trying to make up her mind to a course of action. He raised his eyes from his drink and touched the edge of her gaze as it slipped away. He continued to watch her as she accepted her drink from the waiter and fished in a large, worn handbag for her cigarettes. Her eyes moved up to catch and hold his as she lit her cigarette.

"Sorry to keep you waiting," Sessena said dropping down beside him. "I feel better now that I've unwound a bit."

"You're either too late or too early," Scott said, downing the rest of his drink. "I'm not sure which."

"Did I interrupt something?"

"I don't know. Probably not. You want a drink here?"

"No. I might as well drink Hungarian booze since I'm eating their food. The one might be an antidote for the other."

Scott laid a bill on the check before him. "Let's go. It's in the neighborhood. We can walk."

They walked around the corner of the hotel building and into *Karntnerstrasse*. Light from the shop windows flooded the sidewalk, illuminating in multiple colors the snow piled along the curbing. Traffic moved slowly along the congested street. Flurries of light snow filled the air and, stirred by a sudden wind, stung their eyelids.

"According to the calendar it's spring." Sessena turned up the collar of his coat.

"You'll wake up one of these mornings and spring weather will be here. It's like that in Austria. When it comes, you won't believe it."

"I'll buy that."

They entered the warmth of the restaurant under a sign that said *Pataky, Hungaria Restaurant, Zigeuner Musik*. It was early. A single elderly man was stolidly eating his supper at a table in the corner. They chose a table at the opposite side of the room and ordered *gulyas* and Hungarian tokay wine. A violinist in a worn black suit and a white shirt with a black string tie began to play gypsy airs. They were sad and haunting with a slow, mournful tempo.

"Kind of a waste of atmosphere," Sessena said dourly, "unless this is a hangout for queers."

"It's early. The music gets gayer later when the place fills up and the cash register begins to jingle."

Sessena lit a cigarette. "I'm over here in the role of Fenwick's next of kin, Scottie. A cousin. We'll go down to the Tyrol and claim the body. You are along as an

.12.

American Embassy attaché trying to be helpful to a bereaved American citizen. We'll get as much information as we can from the locals, which won't be much, ship the body back to the States, and blow the place. Sound O.K.?"

Scott nodded. "It's a beginning, and we've got to have a beginning. We'll take a plane down to Innsbruck in the morning. We can rent a car there for the drive down the valley to Zirl where Fenwick's body was found."

Zirl was the kind of small, peaceful Austrian village where flowers bloomed in window boxes in summer and milk carts bounced over narrow, cobbled streets. In March the window boxes were empty above the carved red hearts and stag heads that decorated them and the streets, swept by a raw, blustery wind, were deserted. Scott and Sessena had driven down the Inn Valley to Zirl among the towering, snow-covered Alpine peaks which rose on either side as bulwarks leading to the Italian frontier to the south and the German frontier to the north. The valley had been touched gently and tentatively with the first green of coming spring and outside of the whitewashed building that housed both the post office and the gendarmery a few crocus were in bloom. A wooden stairway rose at the side of the building to a battered wooden door over which hung a faded replica of the state seal of the Republic of Austria. Inside, three men in uniform were sitting in chairs around a stove with a low fire. They stopped talking as the two Americans entered and looked at them curiously.

"Constable Kurtz?" Scott asked.

A well-built, weathered man arose from his chair with a smile. *"Ja, bitte."*

"I'm Scott from the American Embassy in Vienna. I telephoned you from Innsbruck."

"Ja, ja, zehr gut." Kurtz glanced at the other two men in uniform, dismissing them. They arose and left the small room. As the clatter of their heavy boots on the wooden stairway died away, Kurtz motioned his visitors into the vacant chairs. He opened a wooden cabinet and took down a bottle and three small glasses. Very methodically he filled each glass and handed one to Sessena and another to Scott. He raised his own in their direction and then drained it in a gulp. *"Kirschwasser. Zehr gut.* You know it?" he added in English.

"Yes," Scott nodded, looking at the glass appreciatively. "Though we usually drink a sweeter cherry brandy in the States." He nodded to Sessena. "This is a cousin of the dead man, Mr. Kurtz. He is the next of kin and has just come from America to claim the body."

"Ah, so. Just so," Kurtz said looking sympathetically at Sessena. "My condolences, Herr Sessena."

"Thanks," Sessena said laconically.

"We will claim the body this afternoon at the mortuary in Innsbruck and arrange to have it shipped to the United States, but Mr. Sessena understandably would like to know any of the details of the death."

"Of course, *servus*," Kurtz murmured politely. He poured more Kirsch into the glasses, and narrowed his eyes as he looked into the middle distance. "We have had since yesterday photographers, magazine writers, railroad police, and police from Innsbruck and Vienna. I can tell you, they have kept me busy." He rubbed his nose with a forefinger. "I am, after all, only a provincial policeman into whose district the body fell. Since the place the murder occurred was on wheels, the train went on to Basle. It makes it difficult, Herr Sessena. I have the body briefly, but nothing else. All of the clues and the suspects are scattered to the four winds after crossing an international frontier."

"There were no clues?" Sessena asked.

Kurtz shook his head slowly. "When a sparrow falls from the sky, God knows why it falls, but who else? Your cousin, *mein Herr,* he was never in Zirl alive. He had no roots here, no enemies, no friends. We only know of him what we are told. He falls from the Wiener Waltzer Express in his trousers, barefoot and in his undershirt. His body rolls down an embankment near Zirl. It is the merest coincidence, but immediately the world comes awake and says, 'You there, Kurtz, you Constable of gendarmery at Zirl, what happened?' *Mein Gott,* with due respect, *Herren,* how do I know what happened? I am the last to know." He filled his glass from the bottle.

.15.

Sessena glanced briefly at Scott, a flicker of amusement in his eyes.

"Can you show us where the body was found?" Scott asked.

"*Natürlich!* Of course." Kurtz got out of his chair with a suggestion of relief. "It is a short walk. The weather is good."

They walked a short distance through the village and scrambled up an embankment onto the track. It stretched away into the distance, cold, taut, shimmering impersonally in the bright sunlight. "It is about two kilometers from here," Kurtz said.

The three men walked along, stepping from railroad tie to railroad tie. The wind sang in the telegraph wires alongside the track, otherwise all was silence. Kurtz began to look for a marker. He found a stake with a red swatch of cloth tied to it and stopped. "You see, *meine Herren*, from the stop at Innsbruck the trains rapidly pick up speed. At this point they are traveling nearly one hundred kilometers an hour. No one could survive a fall here from a train going so fast." He looked at them intently. "The body fell here, so. Then it rolled forward and down the embankment. We found it in that ditch." His finger jabbed into the distance.

"You said it was murder," Sessena murmured. "Why do you say that? Couldn't it have been an accident?"

"*Nein. Nein,*" Kurtz said slowly.

"Why not?"

Kurtz shrugged. "Why not? First, he was shaving before he fell. Only half of his face was shaven. Why should he fall out of a train half shaven? Second, all of the train doors were locked and secured at Innsbruck. They aren't easy to open, certainly they don't fall open by accident. No, it was suicide, perhaps, or murder, but not an accident. I ask again do half-shaven men commit suicide? I think not."

"No, it wasn't suicide," Sessena growled, looking down the embankment.

Kurtz spread his hands. "Well, then."

"Were there any wounds on him?" Scott asked.

Kurtz smiled. "No gunshot wounds, Herr Scott. No knife wounds. As for blows," he rocked his head slightly back and forth. "Who knows? He fell from a fast-moving train onto gravel and stone. He was a mass of bruises and wounds. His skull was fractured," he moved his head again. "Who knows? Who knows for sure?"

Scott looked off down the track. "It all looks so peaceful and normal now."

"That is what the poor man's fiancée said," Kurtz nodded morosely.

"His fiancée?" Scott glanced at Sessena.

"*Ja.*" Kurtz took a worn notebook out of a pocket of his jacket and wetting a forefinger with his tongue turned the pages. "*Ja,*" he said again with satisfaction, "A fraulein Lani Evron. An exotic name, no? Not Aus-

.17.

trian, surely. She appeared here only this morning."

"Where is she now?" Scott asked.

"I think she returned to Innsbruck." He glanced again at his notebook. "She is staying at the Goldner Hirsch. That is your hotel as well, is it not? Then this is a happy coincidence, no? The poor fraulein was most disturbed. She will be consoled by meeting someone like you, Herr Sessena, who is almost a cousin."

Sessena thoughtfully put a stick of chewing gum in his mouth. "Yeah. It's a small world."

.2.

Scott and Sessena stood in the cold, antiseptic surroundings of the mortuary preparation room in Innsbruck and gazed somberly down upon the body of
Ralph Fenwick that lay nude on a waist-high, narrow
portable trolley. The body was covered with a heavy
green wax in preparation for shipment. Under the
stark light of the unshielded light bulbs hanging from
the ceiling it looked more like a wax figure from a
chamber of horrors than the body of a human being.

The owner of the mortuary was wearing a white
smock, giving the impression in the austere atmosphere
of the small room that he was a surgeon rather than a
mortician. He smiled sadly at Sessena. "I am sorry,
mein Herr. Ordinarily, I would have your cousin dressed
and, with cosmetics and the right lights, he would look
more natural to you. But," he shrugged, "the shipping
regulations require the wax and Herr Scott requires
that he see everything that goes into the coffin before
he seals it, so I have no choice."

"That's O.K.," Sessena said.

"It will all appear differently at the funeral in
America."

"Yeah. I know."

"Shall I prepare the body for shipment, Herr Scott?"

Scott glanced at Sessena, who gave an offhand wave of one hand, then said, "Yes, go ahead."

The mortician summoned an assistant and began to wrap the body in a shroud. They then lifted it into a stout, tight-fitting wooden box and waited expectantly for Scott. Scott ran his fingers perfunctorily across the body and around the edge of the coffin and nodded. The mortician lifted the wooden top of the box into place and the assistant fastened it down with a series of brass screws counter set into the wood. Scott produced a candle, lit it, and let wax drip into a screw hole until it filled to overflowing. He then pressed the seal of the United States into the hot wax. He repeated this laboriously at each of the twenty screw holes, swearing under his breath when the hot wax burnt his fingers. He handed a consular shipping certificate printed on heavy semi-stiff paper to the mortician who tacked it onto the coffin. Scott placed two puddles of wax at opposite corners of the paper and again impressed the seal.

The mortician reached over to a small desk in the corner. "I have a bill," he looked at Sessena mournfully. "I am sorry, but under the circumstances. . . ."

Sessena glanced at the bill. It was in dollars. He wrote a check and handed it to the mortician. The mortician glanced at the check dubiously. "Herr Scott, perhaps, if the Embassy? You understand in the circumstances?"

Scott took the check and wrote in the lower left hand corner, "Payment guaranteed by the United States Embassy in Vienna" and signed his name.

The mortician was satisfied. "*Danke sehr, danke sehr.* You understand, Herr Sessena? It is not personal, only good business."

"Sure. I should have been carrying my credit card." Sessena nodded at Scott. "O.K., Mr. Diplomat. Let's go get a drink."

They opened a heavy mahogany door off the lobby of the Goldner Hirsch with a stained glass window bearing in old German script the word "Ratskeller." A wave of warm air, rich with the mingled odors of cooking food, beer, and wine engulfed them. The owner, dressed in a green Tyrolean suit with carved bone ornaments in the lapels, led them across the smokey room with its low ceiling and heavy beams to a table set in the bow of leaded windows. They ignored the menu placed before them and ordered steins of beer.

Sessena took several deep draughts before he spoke. "It didn't look much like Fenwick, did it?"

"No."

"Only the red hair looked natural. A wax green corpse with red hair." Sessena shook his head and gave a dry, mirthless chuckle. "It was like something on the Late Show."

Scott looked into his beer. "Fenwick was a bit of a ladies' man. There wasn't much left of that."

"Not a damn thing." Sessena glanced at him. "You did that wax seal bit very deftly. Don't tell me you have to seal and stamp every American corpse that leaves Austria as a part of your cover?"

"No. The consulate does that. One of the vice-consuls gave me the kit and instructions so I'd have an excuse to come down here." They had another beer and ordered a meal of wurst and red cabbage.

"What do you think this means, Scottie?"

"I think he was running. Why or where I have no idea."

"Ever hear of this Lani Evron? This fiancée that beat us to the scene of the crime?"

Scott cut very carefully into a piece of wurst and forked it into his mouth. "Fenwick mentioned her once or twice as a girl friend. I doubt he ever formalized it by making a decent proposal."

"What kind of a woman is she?"

"Israeli. Came to Bucharest with a dance troupe and stayed on. I understand she sings at one of the nightclubs out there."

"Could have been a plant."

"It probably was. Fenwick realized that, but he liked what he was getting and thought he could handle it."

"Poor butterfly or a faded flower?"

"Neither. She's twenty-two and Fenwick claimed she was quite a dish."

"I don't like it."

"Neither do I, in retrospect, and I don't like it worth a damn that she has already appeared on the scene. She may have been on that train."

"You are aware of Fenwick's anti-Israeli bias in his latest reports?"

"Yes."

"Hardly goes with shacking up with a beautiful Israeli dame that just happens to get stranded in Bucharest, does it?"

"Unless the reports were true and she was a source of information."

"In that case she would have gotten it, not Fenwick."

"You think the Israelis did it?"

Sessena sipped his beer. "I don't think anything at this point, but I'm mighty curious about this gal. You'd better check that one out thoroughly."

"No strain."

Sessena grinned. "I didn't think there would be, but remember what happened to Fenwick."

"I never ride trains."

Sessena concentrated on his wurst and cabbage. He seemed to have run out of conversation. With his coffee he lit a cigarette and sat looking pensively at Scott through the curling wreath of smoke.

"You look like a normal, uncomplicated guy, Scottie, that ought to be coaching football at some nice little college in the Mississippi River Valley. How did you ever get into this business?"

Scott looked at him in surprise. "Is that a serious question?"

"Yes."

A freckled hand moved through the sandy hair self-consciously. "I'm kind of a throwback, Ernie," he said slowly, "a volunteer, the kind of guy who used to hear the drums and the bugles and see the flag flying and rush to enlist at forty dollars a month with a lump in his throat."

"That's out of style. They call your type suckers nowadays. You going to make a career of it?"

Scott slowly shook his head. "Even cold wars don't last forever. I'll hang out that shingle in Indiana eventually."

"This one's lasted over twenty-five years."

"Maybe I'll chicken out."

"Maybe you will." Sessena sipped his coffee. "You put it very well, Scottie. I wondered what your motivation was. Old bastards like me get kneed, fouled, and gouged all the time and we knee, foul, and gouge right back. We know there's an easier way to make a living and we know in our gut that we have a good reason for what we do, but it takes a guy like you to put it into words. They'll bury Fenwick and forget him. If we're lucky it won't make more than the local newspapers, yet maybe it will turn out that the guy deserved the

Medal of Honor for manning the intelligence parapet in Bucharest as much as a soldier might deserve it for fighting to the end in an advanced salient of the fighting front."

Scott laughed. "We're more likely to get the finger than the Medal of Honor."

Sessena pushed out his cigarette. "Ain't it the truth?" He yawned. "I think I'll turn in early. I'm flying back to the States in the morning. Follow this thing through, Scottie. We've got to know what this Fenwick death means and know it damn fast. He may have been playing it cute and have compromised others, including you. Keep in touch in the usual way. If you need me, give a holler and I'll be back and contact you." He squeezed Scott's shoulder as he arose and headed for the door.

The Goldner Hirsch reception desk told Scott that Miss Evron had been registered, but had checked out late in the afternoon. She had left no forwarding address. Fortunately, with the help of a generous tip, the telephone operator remembered that she had made a reservation at the Kaiserhof at Badgastein.

He drove the rented automobile up the Inn Valley toward Badgastein the next morning. Riding up over a low saddle of land he dropped into the valley of Gastein and drove southward until he saw the pastel hotels of the famous spa strung like a necklace along green alpine foothills that merged abruptly into the snow-covered peaks dividing Austria from Italy.

The resort was between seasons. Only a few of the winter skiers remained and the brisk winds from the surrounding peaks were still too cold to attract the visitors who would arrive in late spring and summer. Scott drove down the narrow street between the rows of hotels and spas, past the roaring cascade of *Wilbad Gastein und Wasserfall,* around the old church and stopped before the ornate and rococo exterior of the Kaiserhof.

He registered and followed the porter to his room. He knew Lani Evron's general appearance from pictures Fenwick had once shown him of a holiday they had taken together at Mamaia on the Black Sea. The best approach was to drift about the hotel and village until he met her. If she had an escort, that would make it more difficult. But she had been alone in Innsbruck.

After glancing into the empty barroom he lunched in the hotel dining room with its great windows overlooking the valley. Then he walked toward the village, stopping to gaze in shop windows and to inspect book stalls while noticing the faces of the pedestrians who were out strolling in the early spring sunshine. It was a day of bright sun and practically no movement of air. The red and white flags and banners of Austria that usually fluttered and swung in the mountain breezes of summer or snapped and whipped in the stronger winds of the other seasons hung limp and flaccid.

Scott stopped on the stone bridge just beyond the

Straubiner Hof and watched the waterfall cascade down from the mountain peaks to plunge beneath the bridge in a wild cloud of spray. A cool mist rose into his face. As he stood there, a tall, slim girl strode past him, her brown, sunstreaked hair with its leonine effect moving restlessly on her shoulders. Her hands were thrust into the deep pockets of a cinnamon-colored suede coat and her eyes were fixed in the middle distance. His heart leaped. It was Lani Evron.

He casually followed her, until the narrow street opened into the Koncert Platz. She had sat down at a small table among old, heavily-pruned sycamores in an area served by a small restaurant. As he approached, she was lighting a cigarette. At the sound of his footfalls on the gravel, her eyes darted up and now fixed him with an alert, appraising look as she continued to hold the lighted match to the cigarette end.

He smiled. "Miss Evron? I am Robert Scott, an old friend of Ralph Fenwick."

She continued to look at him as she waved out the match and let it fall. "You know that he is dead?" Her voice was husky.

"Yes."

She looked away indifferently.

"May I sit down?"

"If you wish."

A waiter appeared and she ordered coffee, ignoring Scott. "A kaffee for me also," he said.

Her wide-set hazel eyes were sad as they returned to

study him. He noticed dark shadows under them and wondered if they were always there. "What do you want of me?" she asked.

"I am with the American Embassy in Vienna. Ralph and I were friends as well as colleagues. I understand that you visited the place where he fell from the train. I thought perhaps you could tell me something about it . . . for the next of kin."

A ghost of a smile which touched her generous mouth did not extend to the steady eyes. She did not speak but nodded in wry acknowledgment of what he had said. They were silent as the waiter served their coffee and crunched back over the gravel in squeaky shoes toward the warmth of the cafe.

"Were you on the train with him?"

"I was on the train," she said slowly in a resigned voice. "I was not with him. He was traveling alone in a locked compartment."

"Do you know why?"

Her eyes flashed. "Of course I know why. He was afraid. He was running for his life."

"From whom?"

She moved her shoulders in a disconsolate gesture. "I don't know."

"Why were you on the train?"

"I wanted to be near him."

She took another cigarette out of her handbag. She let him light it for her. "You knew nothing of this trip?" she asked.

"No. When I heard of his death, I thought he was still in Bucharest."

She shrugged and looked sadly away. "It doesn't matter."

"Were you in love with him?"

The fine eyes came back to him. "That doesn't matter either, does it?"

"I suppose not." He thought of the green wax mummy with the red hair.

She stirred in her chair as if to go.

"Why are you in Badgastein?"

"It is a beautiful spot and was nearby. I wanted some days to rest, to think. Why are you here?"

"I followed you."

"That sounds almost romantic the way you say it; not menacing at all."

He smiled. "I'm not the menacing kind. I have to return to Vienna in the morning. Let me take you to dinner tonight."

For the first time she laughed, showing strong, even white teeth. Her tongue moved across her upper lip as she studied him. "This is what is called a 'pickup' in America?"

"Almost. Not quite."

Her head tipped to one side slightly as she regarded him with a broadening smile that had finally reached her eyes. "All right, Robert Scott. With you, I'll go to dinner."

"Great! Seven o'clock?"

"Yes, seven." She continued to smile at him and then arose, extending to him a warm hand. *"Shalom,"* she murmured, turning away.

They met for cocktails in the small bar of the Kaiserhof and took a horse-drawn carriage out into the countryside for a dinner by candlelight at the Grüner Baum. They danced together to music of a trio and promised to see one another in Vienna. She told him to telephone her at Sachers. When she kissed him good night her lips were warm and yielding. It was hard to remember that she might have killed Ralph Fenwick.

.3.

He left the rental car in Salzburg the next morning and flew to Vienna. As he entered the American Embassy, the Ambassador was descending the broad staircase leading to the street-level lobby. The patrician features regarded him with the tentative expression of half recognition he had learned was characteristic as they met halfway up the stairs.

"Scott?"

"Yes, Sir, Robert Scott."

"I heard about Fenwick."

"Yes, Sir."

"Nasty business. You on top of it?"

"We're doing our best."

"Sure you are. Anything I need to know?"

"Our investigation isn't complete. We will keep you fully informed."

"Don't believe I'd like that. You fellows handle it. Accident, wasn't it?"

"We know nothing that proves to the contrary."

The Ambassador nodded and paused again after descending two steps. "No affair this post. I told the press boys no comment required by me. Keep it out of the newspapers. Cooperate with the local police. Keep 'em happy."

"Yes, Sir."

The Ambassador stared at the electric-blue carpeting on the staircase for a moment. "Silly damn color carpet for an Embassy. Better suited to a bordello. Told 'em that in Washington. Didn't mince any words either." He hesitated and then continued down the staircase.

Scott entered the small, sparsely furnished office on the fourth floor. A slip of white note paper protruded from the edge of the leather blotter frame on his desk. He unfolded it and after glancing at the familiar scrawl across its face, dialed an Embassy extension number.

"Browne?"

"I'll be right in."

A dark, intense man in his middle thirties entered the office and smiled perfunctorily. "Enjoy the mountains?"

"Great."

"No real news here, but I thought you would like to know that a woman called here three times. She used the blue line number rather than the Embassy switchboard."

Scott's brow knitted. "Did she give an identification?"

"None that I recognized." Browne handed him a telephone number. "She asked you to contact her as soon as you could. Said it was urgent."

"Will do." He nodded at Browne and after the door closed behind him dialed the number.

"*Bitte?*"

"I was asked to telephone this number."

"Oh, thank you," the voice grew stronger and its Slavic intonation became more pronounced. "It is very important that I see you very soon."

"Why?"

There was a slight hesitation. "I know about the accident. I may be able to help you."

"Where can I see you?"

"Perhaps you remember me. You were drinking alone at a hotel bar the night before last and a single woman entered?"

"Yes. I remember."

A warm little laugh came over the telephone. "You see? It is not yet too late for me."

"No. It isn't too late."

"You are gallant. Meet me at that same place at five this afternoon. Can you do that?" The question was asked anxiously.

"Yes."

"*Auf Wiedersehen.*"

The telephone clicked softly. Scott stared at the receiver for a moment after he had replaced it in its cradle. He wouldn't pass up a chance to meet a strange woman who had the blue line number.

She was waiting for him at a table in the corner with

.33.

a sherry before her. When she smiled at him she seemed more sensuous than he remembered her. "Thank you for coming."

He acknowledged her comment with an unsmiling nod of the head and sat down beside her.

"I am Magda Stanescu."

"Miss?" he asked gravely.

"Yes, Miss. Would you like a drink?" she asked as the waiter approached. Scott ordered a scotch and soda. When he had been served he lit a cigarette and frankly studied the woman across the table from him. She submitted to his scrutiny without embarrassment, her gray eyes meeting his steadily.

"Where did you get that telephone number?"

"From Ralph Fenwick. He told me to use it only in an emergency."

"Fenwick wouldn't have given you that number."

"But he did."

"Why should I believe that?"

She gave a little shrug and smiled plaintively. "Because it is true. No other reason."

"Convince me it is true."

"First I must convince you that I am Magda Stanescu." She handed Scott a worn passport. He glanced at it briefly and gave it back to her.

"You are Austrian?"

"Yes. Since twelve years. I was born in Transylvania after it became Romanian. My father was an official of the old empire. We are not ethnic Germans but we have always regarded Vienna as our true capital, not Bucharest. When the chance came, I became Austrian. After the state treaty it seemed that at last Austria must be free."

"You do not like the Russians?"

She made a little face. "I understand the Russians. I do not like the Communists. If both Romania and Austria had been Communistic I might as well have remained Romanian."

"Are you a spinster or a widow?"

She pouted faintly. "You are very curious, no? And not very tactful. Why don't you ask me about Ralph Fenwick?"

"We'll get to him. First, I have to make up my mind about you."

She shrugged. "I have had two husbands, both dead, and several lovers. I am a woman of the Balkans and of my time. It is not a time of consistency and of lasting alliances." A faint flush touched her cheeks and she looked at him coquettishly. "As an American you don't understand that, do you?"

He smiled noncommittally. "Where did you meet Ralph Fenwick?"

"Here in Vienna."

"When?"

"Last year, in the spring."

"It sounds romantic."

"I suppose it was," she murmured. "I hadn't thought about it."

"How did you meet him?"

"We were alone in the Prater one Sunday. We began to talk as we waited in line to ride the ferris wheel and we became friends. In time, very good friends."

"He was one of your lovers?"

"I have my lovers one at a time, Mr. Scott," Magda Stanescu spoke evenly, "not in pairs or groups. As a matter of fact, he was not my lover. He was more than that. He was a true friend, a benefactor."

Scott offered her a cigarette and lit it before lighting his own.

She watched him, a little smile playing about her lips. "I am always amazed at you American officials. You are so young, so untouched, so gay; even when you try to be serious, you know, it is all like a game, a not very important game. I find it charming, disarming. European officials are not like that."

"You mean we Americans are naïve."

"No. You are not naïve. That I do not believe."

"Thank you."

"You did not know about me?"

Scott slowly shook his head.

"You should have, you know."

"Fenwick's private life was his own."

"Really? How very nice!" This time a soft laugh bubbled forth.

"You said Fenwick was a benefactor."

Her face saddened and suddenly looked older and heavier. Her voice dropped. "He helped me, helped me greatly, in moving persons from the East to the West."

"For whom?"

"For no one. I believe that people should be free to travel, to live where they choose, particularly if they feel oppressed where they are. I operate what you Americans call an underground railway. Hundreds of persons in Eastern Europe move to the West each month; before Berlin was closed to them by the Wall the number was in the thousands. I help a few each month, perhaps a score when all goes well. I do it through friends. We have no organization, no funds, no political purpose. We are just human beings assisting other human beings. Because we are not doctrinaire, we have never lost a person." Her voice held a note of pride. "Ralph Fenwick was one of those friends. In recent months he became almost indispensable."

Scott's face was expressionless. "Why do you think he helped you, a stranger he met in the Prater on a lonely Sunday?"

"He was a good man."

"How do you choose your refugees?"

"They choose us. We have no requirements other than need. The great, the humble, the young or the old. They all have a right to live where they wish."

"You have no political requirements?"

"None, though I suppose if a person wishes to leave

Eastern Europe for Western Europe or America, they do not like Communism."

"I suppose so." Scott put out his cigarette. "You don't investigate these people you help? You may be infiltrated and betrayed or used."

Magda Stanescu slowly shook her head. "It has never happened. It never will happen. All of our refugees are recommended by others who have gone. We are like a large family. We deal only with individuals; we are at the human, personal level. At that level, people are good, Mr. Scott. They are trustworthy, loyal, grateful. It is only when doctrine and bureaucracy impersonalize human relationships that people become cruel."

"Someone was cruel to Ralph Fenwick."

"Yes," she agreed somberly.

"You said to me on the telephone that you knew something about his death."

"Yes. I was on the train from which he fell."

Scott waited.

"He was not himself, Mr. Scott. Since his murder I have asked myself, was it fear? Was it a premonition? No, how can I say it in English? He was disorganized, distraught."

"Were you traveling with him?"

"No. I boarded the train here in Vienna. I had an appointment in Zürich. In the corridor of the train I met Franz, a waiter from the dining room of this hotel. You can imagine my surprise. He is one of my friends in the underground railway. Ralph had sent him from the train for a bottle of whiskey and sandwiches. It waits in Vienna after arrival from the East nearly an hour. Franz gave me the compartment number. I knocked on the compartment door. Ralph was not happy to see me. He was unshaven, gruff, preoccupied, rude. He asked to be left alone. I was deeply hurt, no? We are good friends and he acts like this." She looked at Scott sadly. "I did not see him again, but later I saw a woman enter his compartment."

"Did you recognize who it was?"

"Not then. I had just entered one end of the carriage on my way through to the dining car when I saw this figure enter Ralph's compartment at the other end."

"Are you certain this person entered Fenwick's compartment?"

"Yes. I walked down to it and listened at the door. Really, Mr. Scott, I am quite shameless when I am curious and I was curious about the well-being of a friend. You understand?"

"I'm sure Ralph forgives you," Scott said dryly.

"I heard a woman's voice. It was the voice of Lani Evron, his mistress in Bucharest."

"You knew he had a mistress?"

She smiled and spread her hands. "We were friends. Good friends, but not lovers. I had no jealousy. I knew of his mistress. Why not? Often we talked of many things. I was like a sister to him. He was too kind to make me feel like a mother and I was not that much older. She is a Jewess. Later I observed that she was traveling with friends, maybe bodyguards, and that she was being followed and watched by others who I think were not friends. Her name is Lani Evron," she repeated.

"You are very observant."

"I have learned to be."

"Why are you telling this to me?"

Magda Stanescu smiled. "If you are the wrong person for me to speak to, then tell it to the one who should hear what I have said, but I don't think I have made a mistake, Robert Scott; I think you are the right person." Her eyes looked into his shrewdly.

"Where can I find you later?"

She reached into her purse and gave him a card with a telephone number on it. "I don't like to meet foreign agents in public. This was unavoidable. That telephone number is inverted. Dial it from right to left and I will receive your message."

"I thought you trusted people?"

"I trust the uncommitted. It is the idealists who kill impersonally, Mr. Scott, did you know that? Unfortunately, Vienna is filled with idealists of all persuasions these days. They stalk about with their guns and bombs, filled with an impersonal love for humanity, performing their daily task of killing human beings one by one in the name of humanitarianism. Be wary. Be alert. Relax only with the uncommitted." She shook his hand gravely and left him.

.4.

Scott had another drink before leaving the barroom. He walked across the lobby to the entrance to the dining room. It was too early for diners, but the headwaiter was overseeing his staff as they set the tables with glistening white damask tablecloths, silver, crystal, and flowers. He stepped over to Scott. *"Mein Herr?"* he murmured politely.

"I should like to speak with your waiter named Franz."

A faint look of distress touched the otherwise professionally composed face. "That is rather irregular, *mein Herr.* Is it not possible for you to see him elsewhere?"

Scott pressed a bill into his hand. "No. I must see him now. It is urgent."

The headwaiter slightly inclined his head in resigned assent. "Franz the elder or Franz the younger?"

"Franz the elder," Scott made a guess.

"Come this way please."

He led Scott through serving doors into the immaculate white porcelain and stainless steel kitchen. The noise and activity in the kitchen as the chefs prepared for the dinner hour contrasted with the calm of the still empty and half-lit dining room. *"Bitte.* Wait here for a moment." The headwaiter disappeared among the steam kettles and glowing ovens. He soon returned with a placid-faced, slightly stooped waiter with a ruff of gray-white hair about a pale, bald head. "Franz," the headwaiter said in a peremptory tone, "this is the gentleman that wished to speak with you." He gave a little bow in Scott's direction and disappeared through the serving door into the dining room.

Franz looked at Scott, a tentative little smile on his lips. He spoke below the noise level in the busy kitchen. "What can I do for you, *mein Herr?*" He stood quietly, his hands folded before him.

"I am Robert Scott of the American Embassy. I understand that you knew my colleague Ralph Fenwick."

Franz's pleasant, indefinite expression did not change. "Why do you assume that, Herr Scott?"

"Magda Stanescu told me so."

Franz wet his lips. "No offense, Herr Scott, but do you have some identification?"

Scott showed him an Embassy pass.

"Yes. I knew Herr Fenwick. I am sorry about his death."

"When did you last see him?"

"A few days ago when his train was in Vienna, the very train from which he fell. He sent to me and asked me to bring a bottle of scotch and some chicken sandwiches to his compartment. I was glad to do it."

"He seemed in good spirits?"

"A little strained, a little tired. He told me that is why he didn't wish to leave his compartment. I told him that he shouldn't work so hard."

"Was he traveling alone?"

"It appeared so. Yes."

"Do you think he was afraid to leave his compartment?"

Franz's eyes had an opaque look. "I have no reason to believe so, Herr Scott. I took him at his word."

Scott thrust a bill toward Franz. "Thank you very much for your cooperation."

The waiter firmly rejected the bill. "That is not necessary, Herr Scott. I am glad to have been of service."

Scott withdrew his hand. "I do thank you."

"Servus," Franz gave a grave little bow.

Scott telephoned the Hotel Sacher and asked for Lani Evron. She had not yet arrived. He left a message for her to call him with the telephone number of his apartment. She rang him up the next morning. "I am glad you remembered," the voice was lower and more sensual than he recalled it.

"You knew that I would remember."

"Yes, perhaps, but we can't always have things as we wish."

"May I see you?"

"Yes, of course. I have only spent the night at Sachers. I am checking out now. A friend has given me the use of a small apartment for a few days. Let me give you lunch there, latish, since I must orient myself first in a strange kitchen."

"Two o'clock?"

"Perfect." She gave him an address on a curving street in the Innerstadt not far from the Danube Canal.

The ancient elevator imprisoned in a wrought iron cage was not working and he walked up a chilly, twisting, stone staircase to the apartment landing. He pushed the bell button with a forefinger. After a short interval Lani Evron opened the heavy black oak door and smiled across the threshold at him radiantly. She wore a simple frock in bright yellow and brushed her hair back with one hand in an unconscious gesture as she greeted him.

"How very nice."

He took her extended hand with a thrill of pleasure he had not anticipated and returned her smile. "It's going to be a good day."

"A happy day?"

"I'm sure of it."

The apartment had been created with three others from the spacious floor plan of a pre-World War I apartment. There was the one large, high-ceilinged room, which they had now entered from the small vestibule, overlooking the street with a glimpse of the canal and its park at the end, a tiny but modern kitchen, and one rather small, dark bedroom. The furniture, comfortable rather than smart, was a combination of new and traditional Austrian designs. There were two rather fine pieces, a carved walnut chest and a rosewood table with an intricate inlay.

"Very chic," he said.

"The owner has gone to Paris for a few days. I feel very lucky. It is so much better than the hotel."

"I agree."

"Would you like a sherry?"

"Very much."

She poured wine for each of them and sat down on a small sofa opposite him, tucking one leg under her. "I am so glad you telephoned."

"So am I."

"I was afraid you wouldn't."

"You can gauge your effect on me better than that."

Her smile was disingenuous. "Do I have an effect?"

"Terrific."

She laughed a light, warm laugh. "Good. Every girl likes to hear that." She sipped her sherry, her eyes dropping to the edge of the glass. When she raised them she was more serious. "I am glad, though, Bob. I truly am. I'm rather at loose ends at the moment. It's good to have a new friend, possibly a very good new friend."

"Will you stay in Vienna?"

Her eyes were doe-like. "Would you like me to?"

"Yes."

"Then I will. There is no reason for me to go back to Bucharest."

"What did you do in Bucharest?"

"I sang in a supper club there. I am really a dancer."

"Classical or modern?"

"Both. I prefer the ballet. That is what I studied in Tel Aviv."

"Why Bucharest?"

"I very foolishly joined an international dance troupe. I thought it was my big opportunity. It ran out of money and broke up in Bucharest. I was stranded. So I did what I had to do."

"I understand."

"I hope you really do," she looked at him earnestly.

"We all do what we have to do."

"I know," she said pensively. "That is when childhood ends, they used to say in Israel."

He turned his glass, letting the sunlight glow in the amber liquid. "Did you ever know Magda Stanescu in Bucharest?"

She was very still, then she answered quietly. "No. Should I have?"

"Not at all. She just happens to be the only Romanian I know. One always asks such things."

"Would you like more sherry?"

"Yes, thank you."

"I shall fill your glass and have mine in the kitchen

while I prepare our luncheon. It will be simple and quick."

"Good. I'd rather have your company than your food."

She filled his glass and lightly touched his cheek with her fingertips. "I am so pleased that you are here," she murmured as she turned away.

The luncheon was a light, airy omelet and a broiled tomato eaten on a converted table by the window.

"Let's drive up to the Kahlenberg and enjoy the view," he suggested over coffee. "It's a fine, clear day."

She smiled across the table at him and reached for his hand. "Let's."

They drove in the spring sunshine out of the valley of the Danube, through the suburb of Grinzing and into the Vienna woods which covered the hills surrounding Vienna with waves and billows of trees still silent and gray, as yet showing no signs of green. They parked the Opel at the edge of the cobblestone road and followed paths into the woods until in low places the ground underfoot became wet and spongy from the water of the spring thaw and they turned back. At the Kahlenberg they had coffee and Sachertorte in the restaurant and walked out on the terrace as the sun began to set across the city beyond the suburb of Hietzing. The Danube, a small curving ribbon of water in the distance, reflected a faint rose glow as the lights of Vienna winked on.

A cold breeze began to blow, whipping and snapping a row of flags that fluttered from flagstaffs along the balcony. Lani turned up the collar of her green tweed coat with a shiver. "It is beautiful, Bob, but it makes me sad. I prefer the illusion of a smaller world. It makes me feel less insignificant."

"Would you like to go in?"

"Please."

She was still subdued on the drive down the twisting road from the summit. As they reached a straighter portion of the road she moved across the seat until her body touched his. He put his arm around her and she snuggled against him with a contented little sigh. Her fingers fondled his. "You have a strong hand."

"Thank you."

She turned and looked at his profile for a moment with luminous dark eyes and then kissed him lightly on the cheek.

"Would you like to have dinner with me tonight? Somewhere with dancing?" he asked after an interval.

"I would love to."

"I'll drop you off and return about eight."

"Why don't you come home with me? There are men's shaving things in the bathroom cabinet and it would save you two trips across town."

"You aren't tired of my company?"

"Don't be a goose."

She left him in an easy chair with a magazine when she disappeared into the bedroom to change. Reappearing a half hour later in a simple black dress with a flared skirt, she pirouetted before him, her tawny hair sweeping gracefully across her shoulders as she turned.

"You are beautiful."

"You really think so?" Her eyes were shining.

"Yes."

"You really do?"

"Cross my heart."

She leaned over and kissed him on the mouth. "It is a happy day. I knew it would be when I first saw you this morning."

"Shall I freshen up?"

She took him by the hand and led him through the bedroom to the lighted bathroom. "I've laid out everything I think a man needs."

"I'll get along fine."

She blew him a kiss and turned back to the living room.

He stood before the heavy, walnut-framed oval mirror. The etched square glass shades over the light bulbs in brass fixtures on either side of the mirror bathed his tanned face in a flat, white light. He picked up the soap stick and the safety razor that had been placed on the shelf above the lavatory for his use and looked at them quizzically for a moment, holding them before him in his palms as if he were judging their weight. He then shrugged, laid them down again, and removed his jacket, tie, and shirt for his wash up.

They had a light dinner of broiled trout with a green salad and dry white wine in a restaurant off the Opera

Ring and danced to an orchestra that was famous for its slow, romantic tempos. Lani's hair brushed lightly against his face as they danced and her soft cheek was dry and cool against his. They may have been perfumed with a delicacy beyond a male capacity to distinguish or identify, but to Scott they were touched with a suggestion of the day's clean sun and the soft breeze of afternoon.

Their last bottle of wine lay upended in the ice water of the ornate silver wine cooler in its stand by their table and the restaurant was nearly empty when Lani glanced at the small gold watch on her tanned wrist. She looked up with a smile at Scott and caught her lower lip in her teeth in a child's expression of unrepentant naughtiness. "It's deep into the morning, *neshomeleh*. You must take me home."

"*Neshomeleh?*"

"That means darling in my language or *liebling* in German."

"I like the idea in all languages." He glanced regretfully at the orchestra. "They would probably break their instruments if we asked them to play again."

"Yes," she sighed. "It's time to go. It has been a happy day, *liebling*, and an enchanted evening." She picked up her purse and as she arose an attentive waiter hurried over to place her wrap across her shoulders.

"*Danke schoen.*"

"*Bitte, fraulein. Bitte, bitte.*"

.50.

Scott laid some bills on the check and they were bowed from the restaurant into the chill of the Danube mist that enveloped the ornate port-cochere with its semicircle of soft, cream-colored lights in glass globes. The Opel was brought to them by an agile parking attendant and Scott swung into the deserted, shadowed street, leaving the glow of light behind them.

Lani moved close to him as he drove, humming one of the melodies the orchestra had played several times during the evening, but they did not speak, preferring to retain the atmosphere of the restaurant and its music and carry it with them into the dark night.

He stood with her before her door and fitted the heavy key she gave him into the old-fashioned lock. She turned when the door opened and drew him inside. "Stay with me, darling," she whispered. "I don't want to be lonely, and I would be." He gave the door a push with one foot and took her in his arms in the small vestibule as the latch caught the door jamb with a solid, metallic click.

.5.

He went directly to the Embassy the next morning
and telephoned Magda Stanescu, inverting the num-
bers on the card she had given him. "I would like to
talk with you again," he said when she answered.

She sounded sleepy. "It is very early. Are you such
an early riser or have you been up all night?"

"It's a little of both."

"You know the person you talked to after you left
me?"

"Yes. Do you?"

She laughed easily. "He will meet you in the gardens near the Votivkirche at eleven o'clock and will
bring you to me."

"Eleven o'clock. Right."

Franz was wearing a wrinkled black raincoat and a
worn green felt hat. He was walking along the tulip
beds intently inspecting the green shoots that had burst
from the soil. When he saw Scott approaching he casually turned away from him and began to shamble
toward one of the side streets radiating away from the
church and its park. After a few hundred meters he let
Scott overtake him. "Number eighty-seven, apartment
six," he said, as Scott drew abreast. The apartment
building was a short distance beyond and Scott turned

in without hesitation and rang the bell below the white number six on a mottled, blue-enameled plate.

Magda Stanescu was standing at the open door of her apartment smiling at him when he reached her landing by means of the stairs. "Come in. I shall give you coffee for your trouble." The door shut behind them and they moved into a rather dark, overfurnished apartment with the musty odor of age about it. A heavy brass chandelier hanging from the high ceiling was lighted. "We get the afternoon sun," she explained, gesturing that he was to sit on a sofa by a coffee table, "but in the morning it is more cheerful if we use electricity."

She poured coffee from a silver pot of an ornate Victorian design and offered him a light-textured coffee cake with a crumbly topping of brown sugar.

"This is delicious," he said. "It is almost as if you expected me."

"No. We Viennese like our midmorning snack and if we have an unexpected guest, so much the better."

Scott sipped his second cup of coffee. "The more I thought about our conversation the other evening, the more it interested me."

"I should think so," she murmured.

"If true, it means that Fenwick had many personal relationships that went beyond his official duties."

She ignored the implication of his qualification and gazed at him levelly from her wide-set eyes. "I would have thought the information that he was not alone on the train would have most interested you. It seems that you suspect our poor refugees, when you should suspect the Jews."

"No. I don't suspect the refugees. I am just interested in an organization that has the capability of infiltrating agents into the West."

"Don't be ridiculous!" she scoffed. "We do not have that capability." Her eyes snapped. "You think that I would do that for the Communists? What kind of a woman do you think I am?"

"I don't think you would do it consciously, but you could have been used. Fenwick may have used you for that matter."

"I thought you were friends," she said bitterly.

"I am trying to find out the truth."

She lit a cigarette and waved out the match with a nervous gesture. "Let us be frank with one another. Ralph was a diplomatic attaché in Bucharest. You are a diplomatic attaché in Vienna. You were not 'friends' at all. He was a spy and you are a spy." Her mouth twisted. "As a spy, you really trust no one."

Scott sat quietly, steadily meeting her gaze. "If we assume that as a working hypothesis, where does that take us?"

"It should take you to an investigation of Lani Evron and the Israelis. I think they killed Ralph Fenwick. Until you know all about the Jews, you should not try to discredit my little effort to aid refugees."

.55.

"I am not overlooking the Israelis, nor Lani Evron. Have you any more to help me there?"

"Ralph Fenwick had grown to hate them."

"How do you know?"

"I could tell from what he said in casual conversation."

"I thought Lani Evron was his mistress?"

"He was growing tired of her. In a short time that would have ended."

"You think she killed him?"

"It's possible."

"But you don't really believe it?"

"I am not prepared to say what I believe," she said stubbornly.

"Why would the Israelis want to kill Fenwick? The fact that he hated them wouldn't be enough. Over the centuries they have grown used to hate."

Magda Stanescu made a movement with her shoulders. "One never grows used to hate."

"Why do you dislike the Jews?"

Her eyes widened. "I? I don't dislike them. They have had enough trouble, just like the rest of us. I only say that Ralph Fenwick was afraid of them and that they may have killed him."

"I thought you said he hated them."

"That too."

"Yet he had an Israeli mistress," Scott persisted.

"She was a woman, like any other. When he took

her to bed I doubt that he was really interested in her nationality or politics, or religion for that matter."

He smiled. "And you said you were not jealous of her!"

"I was not!" she said hotly.

"Did your refugee group ever help a Jew?"

Her eyes shifted. "They have their own organizations. They don't need my help."

"May I have more coffee? Or do you wish to throw me out?"

She absently poured coffee into his cup, a worried frown on her face. "Let us forget the Jews for a moment. You will learn what you will learn. I am concerned about your suspicions of my group. I can't afford to have you make a hostile report to the United States government. Things are now difficult. That would make them impossible."

"I have no intention of causing you trouble."

"I only approached you because Ralph Fenwick was a dear friend and I want his death avenged."

"Otherwise it has nothing to do with you or your organization?"

"Otherwise, no, I am certain of it."

"I wish that I could be as sure."

Magda Stanescu placed her palms against her cheeks in a gesture of frustration. "I see that I must trust you more, Mr. Scott, to persuade you that your suspicions lie in the wrong quarter." She rose from the sofa and moved to the back of the apartment. In a few minutes she returned with Franz and a stocky blond young man of about twenty-five. "You know Franz. This is Karl. Apart from two couriers in the field you see before you our entire organization."

Scott shook hands with the two men. Franz seemed straighter and taller than he appeared in the Bristol dining room. His handclasp was firm, almost hard, and the hesitant, obsequious manner of the waiter had disappeared. Karl looked at Scott from clear blue eyes set in a deeply tanned face. His movements were controlled and effortless like those of a professional athlete.

Magda Stanescu sat down and motioned for the men to do likewise. "Now, Mr. Scott, let me tell you how we operate." She sensed the stiffening in Franz's attitude. "It is necessary, Franz. Mr. Scott feels that our refugee movement has some responsibility for Ralph Fenwick's death."

"That's impossible," Franz protested.

"We know it is impossible. Mr. Scott does not. That is why I propose to tell him how we operate. He will see for himself how impossible it is."

Franz nodded in reluctant acquiescence.

"Let us remember, Mr. Scott, we have been doing this humanitarian work for some years. It was not always so, but today if there is a person in the East who wishes to come West, he advises a friend or a relative who made the trip with us earlier. That friend or relative contacts me here in Vienna and we give the person who wishes to come West a code number. When it is his turn a field courier contacts him and arranges his trip. That is all there is to it."

"Where does the money come from?"

"We don't need much. Our 'alumni' contribute to us regularly. They feel that they owe their new life to us and they are willing to contribute a share of their earnings to our work."

"How do you arrange for travel documents?"

"We don't. In that sense this is a humanitarian clandestine, illegal operation." She laughed. "I could keep you here all day telling you how we move people across frontiers. We have sent people out in flour barrels, as participants in sports and cultural exchanges, even in uniform during troop maneuvers. Once we sent a small woman West stretched out in the luggage rack of a second-class railway carriage."

"And what about identity papers and visas for the West?"

"We forge them. We are really rather good at it by this time, aren't we Franz?"

Franz gave a deprecating little gesture.

"Don't you see the risk in this, Miss Stanescu?" Scott asked.

"No."

"Can't you see that by this time you may be moving Communist agents exclusively, much more effectively than they could move them themselves?"

"That is not possible," she said confidently. "This is

a human chain of clasped hands. We always have hold of one another in a very real sense."

"Really, Mr. Scott," Franz intervened. "We never deal with strangers."

"And you can trust each other?"

"Franz and I have worked together since 1945 when I was a young girl with a passion for freedom and no sense." She smiled affectionately at Franz who quickly returned the smile. "Franz taught me to distinguish between what is desirable and what is possible. As for Karl," she reached out and clasped his hand, "he is the son of a very dear friend who was not as fortunate as some. I have known him since he was a small boy."

"And Fenwick. You gave him the same trust?"

"Not entirely, though I believe he deserved it."

"Not entirely?"

"He worked as a field courier in the Balkans. He had no need to fully understand the Vienna operation. It was better for him."

"I see." Scott was silent for a moment. "Don't you keep a record of your refugees, names, new names, if any, place of origin, present residence?"

Magda Stanescu hesitated. "No."

"You wouldn't find such a record useful?"

"It would be useless because it would be unnecessary. As I have emphasized before, this is a voluntary movement. Our contributors seek us out to contribute. We hope they are all well and happy in their new life, but we have no need to keep a record of them."

"Has anyone else asked you about such a record?"

"No."

"Ralph Fenwick did, didn't he?" Scott played a hunch.

Magda Stanescu's eyes were opaque. "He did not."

Franz stirred uneasily.

"Franz?" Scott asked.

"Nothing, Sir."

Scott got up from the sofa. "I suggest that you should think about your organization. Is it unreasonable to suppose that among those you have helped West there might not be one who wanted to cover his tracks, to disappear without a trace? If Fenwick was helping such a person West, might not that person have turned on him and destroyed him? Or if you keep records, might not a knowledge of such records be dangerous?"

"We don't keep records," Magda Stanescu insisted stubbornly.

"It's only an idea," he smiled at her. "You gave me one theory for his death. I'm suggesting another. I should think you would want to be certain that no one wishes you ill." He shook hands with Franz and Karl and walked to the door. She opened it for him after removing a chain. "For a humanitarian movement you do seem to take precautions."

"That is because we are in contact with a spy," she said in a low voice, almost whispering the last word. "We don't want to inherit your troubles."

"Heaven forbid," he said.

.6.

Following Lani's suggestion of the night before, Scott bought tickets for *The King with the Umbrella*, playing at a little theatre on *Neubaugasse*, and called for her in a taxi at her apartment a half hour before the performance. When he arrived she was ready wearing a short blue velvet dress with a black coat of silk. She smiled at him gaily. "Have you missed me today, *liebling?*"

"Every minute."

"How nice, because I have thought about you since you left me this morning." She put one arm through his and gave it a little embrace.

They entered the small theatre just as the lights began to dim and the great chandelier which hung in the center of the auditorium and obscured the stage was slowly raised upward toward the rococo reliefs of the vaulted ceiling. The play was laid in the France of Louis Philippe as a comedy of manners, French in concept, but wholly Viennese in execution. They joined in the gales of laughter that swept the theatre at the thrusts and counter-thrusts of the dialogue. Lani seemed to share the play with him physically by a side-wise glance, the movement of her shoulder against his, a light pressure of fingertips on the back of his hand.

There was not a moment that he was unaware that she was beside him.

At the second intermission they smoked cigarettes out on the sidewalk. He reentered the theatre to buy them a refreshment at one of the crowded buffets. It took longer than he had anticipated. The houselights had already blinked once when he returned to the corner of the lobby where they were to meet. She was not there. He stood, a roll and cheese in each hand, waiting for her as the crowd drifted back into the auditorium. Soon he was alone. He looked through the doorway over the heads of the audience now settled for the last act. Their two seats were empty. The usher looked at him inquiringly and with an expression of apology closed the twin padded doors into the theatre. He stood irresolutely in the empty lobby, feeling the chill night air from the darkened street outside flow in around him. After about five minutes he dropped the rolls and cheese into a waste container and lit a cigarette. What the hell? Was he being stood up or had something happened to her? He was finishing his third cigarette when he felt her hand on his arm. "Come, *liebling*," she said. "There is no time to explain."

A black sedan was waiting by the curb. She entered the opened rear door and he followed. The driver, a small man in a dark blue suit, pulled away from the curb and accelerated rapidly down the narrow street as it curved toward *Mariahilferstrasse*.

"Where are we going?" he asked.

"To your apartment. I will explain later."

He looked at her profile lighted by the occasional street lights that flashed by them. Her mouth was set in a firm line, slightly drawn down at the corners by tension. She stared straight ahead, preoccupied with her thoughts.

They braked to an abrupt stop before his starkly modern apartment building on *Josefstaderstrasse*. He followed her up a flight of three stairs from the sidewalk into the small, brightly lit, half-enclosed outer lobby and inserted his key into the pressed wood door leading to the inner lobby. They walked across the small room into a house elevator which was resting at the lobby floor level with its door open, lighted by a single bulb in its ceiling. He pressed a button beside the number four in a small brass plate. The door slid shut. With a jerk the elevator began to ascend.

She preceded him into his apartment after he opened the door. When he switched on the living room light she was standing in the center of the room facing him, her mouth slightly parted, her eyes dark with emotion.

"O.K.," he said shortly. "What is it?"

"Something has gone very wrong. A man has been murdered. He is in your bathroom."

He stared at her a moment as she stood beneath the fluted modernistic parchment shade of the overhead light, then turned and walked through his bedroom into the bathroom. The body lay crumpled up in a corner between the washbasin and the tub. He leaned over it and then murmured, "Thank God there is no blood."

She stood behind him, peering over his shoulder, her face chalky-white.

"What was his name?"

"Stein."

He turned and noticed her paleness. "You'd better have a brandy." He led her back into the living room and poured a splash of the liqueur into a large glass. She took it gratefully. The color slowly flooded back into her face and she sat down in a chair. He poured himself a drink and sat down opposite her. "What was he?"

She hesitated.

"Don't play games with me, Lani," he said harshly. "I want an answer and I can be just as tough as I have to be to get it."

"He was an intelligence officer for Israel." Her voice was barely audible.

"You worked for him?"

"No, I . . . I was helping him."

Scott lit a cigarette and regarded her angrily. "What was this supposed to be? You set me up . . . for what?"

She shook her head miserably and looked at him with wet eyes. "I didn't know. Truly, I didn't. When he observed that you were interested in me he asked me to tell him when we planned to be out together and for how long. That is all I did."

"Unfortunately for Stein someone else decided to visit my apartment at the same time. They both had an exaggerated idea of what it might contain. I don't play the game that way. Everything of importance is locked up in the Embassy, iron bars, heat sensors, combination locks, that sort of thing." He gazed at Lani, "Unless what Stein got was meant for me, in which case I apologize to the State of Israel."

"Please!"

"Stein looked as if he were struck on the head and then strangled. I wouldn't have liked that." He continued to gaze at her speculatively. "You seem familiar with my apartment." The statement was a question.

"Ralph Fenwick brought me here when we were on a visit from Bucharest. You let him use the apartment. You were on home leave."

"I suppose I have to believe that," he said. "I did let him use the apartment."

"Do you think I would tell you that if it weren't true?"

"Yes. I think you might tell me anything."

She bit her lip and looked at the floor. After a moment she spoke in a subdued voice. "We must move the body. He must not be found here."

"We agree on that. Any suggestions?"

"If we can get him into the car trunk, the driver can manage the rest. He knows where to take him."

"It won't be easy to move the body out of here. We'll

be seen if we use the front door and the elevator and there is no rear exit."

She raised her eyes to his. "There is a window in your bathroom that opens into an airshaft. At the bottom of the airshaft is a door connecting it to a service area. We can throw the body down the shaft and lift it into the car trunk from the service area."

"Ralph and you got around," he said drily. He downed the rest of his brandy and returned to the bathroom. He stepped into the tub and opened the casement window which was waist-high and composed of two frosted panes opening out into the airshaft. He leaned out and looked down the shaft. "I think we can do it," he said, turning to Lani. "You will have to help."

"Yes." She took off her pumps and stood in her stockinged feet.

"I'll lift him into the tub and raise him up to the window level. To get him over the sill you will have to push from underneath. I won't have enough leverage."

"I can manage."

Stein was not a big man nor a heavy man, but within the awkward limits of the bathroom it took several minutes to lift the body over the windowsill. It hung for a moment, then plunged feet first down the shaft. The impact of the body striking the pavement below echoed up. Then there was silence.

"Let's go down and claim the remains," Scott said quietly.

They took the elevator down to the street level and instructed the driver to back into the service area behind the building. Scott and the driver carried the body the few feet to the trunk and placed it inside. There was still no blood though both legs had been broken as they twisted under the corpse upon impact with the ground.

The driver nodded a morose farewell and quietly moved the car back into the street. He turned downhill and accelerated away into the night. As the red taillights disappeared into the darkness, Lani drew a tremulous breath. "That is done."

Scott took her firmly by the arm.

"Where are we going?" she asked as he propelled her forward.

"My car is parked near the corner. I want to talk with you and that's the best place to do it."

She accompanied him submissively.

He swung the Opel into Ringstrasse before he spoke.

"What did Stein want in my apartment?"

"How can I answer you?" she asked plaintively. "He told me nothing of his plans."

"Did you 'help' Israeli intelligence in Bucharest too?"

"I am a dancer, not a spy. But I was alone in Bucharest. I needed money and Israel is my country, after all. It was not wrong to help them if they asked and if they were willing to help me with money."

"I'd be the last one to say it was."

"What I do is harmless."

"I am not so sure of that," he spoke drily. "Were you asked to become Fenwick's mistress?"

"I was not his mistress! You are still angry with me. It was not that . . . definite. He did not support me. We were friends."

"Your friends have short lives."

She turned away from him and looked out of the window. Her voice was muffled when she spoke. "I do not sell my affections. You must believe that if you believe nothing else."

"Did Israeli intelligence ask you to cultivate Fenwick?"

"No. I knew Ralph before Israeli intelligence approached me. I suppose that is why they asked me to help them."

"Why were they interested in him?"

"For the same reason they are interested in you, I suppose."

"Will they kill me like they killed Fenwick?"

She looked at him in alarm. "We Israelis did not kill Fenwick! This you must believe. You must!"

"Then you had better start giving me some straight answers. I don't buy this bit about you being an innocent and patriotic amateur. The results are too professional. Why was Israeli intelligence interested in Fenwick? Why were you on that train with him?"

She searched in her bag for a cigarette and lit it very deliberately. "I was told that Ralph was sending false, anti-Israeli reports to the United States," she said slowly. "I was asked to find out why, if I could. My people wanted to know whom he saw, if he seemed to have large amounts of money. They were convinced that someone was buying him, probably the Arabs. If we found out, we intended to inform the United States so that you would remove him from his post and discount his reports."

"And what did you find out?"

"Nothing of that sort. I am not very good at such things. But I became aware in recent weeks that he was not himself."

"He complained about it?"

"No, he didn't. But he was preoccupied, irritable, and, at the last, when he took the train West, afraid."

"Afraid of what?"

"Of himself, I think."

"You think he planned suicide?"

"No. I don't believe that. He was just unaccountable, unpredictable. This deeply worried him. There were parts of days that he could not remember . . . minutes, hours, sometimes. It would become apparent in conversations, then he would become very upset and change the subject."

"So, you followed him West because you were worried about him." The tone was faintly sarcastic.

"I was worried about him. I followed him West because I was told to do so."

"You were the Israeli sex bait for him and now for me?"

She was silent. When she finally spoke, her voice was flat with a little tremor in it. "I must expect things like that to be said, I know."

"It's true, isn't it?" he asked brutally.

She drew a tremulous little breath. "I am a soldier in a nation of soldiers. Women bear the same burdens as the men. I have worked on and guarded a *kibbutz* under the fire of the Arabs. You might admire me for that." Her voice broke. "This work is much harder. Very much harder."

"I'm sorry," he said not unkindly. "I'm in the business. I know how tough it is. I shouldn't give you a hard time just because I now realize that I am only an assignment to you."

"That is not true. You should remember that you sought me out. Besides, my feelings for you are real. If I thought of you only as an American agent I would never have told you of the body when the driver contacted me at the theatre. I would have let you discover it yourself and dispose of it as you could. I would have stayed out of it."

"Not entirely. The body would eventually have been identified as that of Stein, an Israeli agent. You needed me to recover the body and keep the matter quiet. None of us want public attention."

Lani suddenly laughed, breaking the tension. "So, it was that, a little. Maybe we need each other after all."

He grinned for the first time. "I'll still buy your supper, reserving my options, of course."

"Choose some simple place with plain food. I have no appetite."

But when they stopped at a family restaurant in Hietzing they hungrily ate a dish of eggs and sausage from the scrubbed top of a plain wooden table under the flat glare of overhead lights.

"With Stein gone, what do you do now?" Scott asked over coffee.

"I don't know. I wait for instructions," she said, unconsciously dropping her pretense that she was only a penniless dancer. "He was the only Israeli agent in Vienna. The driver has another vocation."

"Is your apartment Stein's?"

"Yes."

"Have you enough money?"

"For now."

"Who do you think killed Stein?"

"You didn't. I didn't. I suppose it could have been anyone else."

"The Arabs?"

"Yes. Very probably."

"The Russians?"

"Yes. Less probably."

"The Americans?"

"Not in your apartment."

"The driver?"

"He discovered the body after Stein didn't reappear at the appointed time."

"He had a convenient opportunity."

"He is a rabbi."

"Oh. Shall I take you home?"

"If you will stay with me."

"My apartment would seem ghoulish, but do I have to use Stein's razor?"

"That is not Stein's razor."

"Oh."

She didn't explain but covered his hand with hers. "Do you still love me after all this?"

"Yes, but I don't trust you."

"That will do."

"I wonder how the play ended?"

"We shall have to find out sometime."

.7.

The telephone rang at midmorning on the Embassy blue line. Scott picked up the receiver and recognized the soft accent of Magda Stanescu. He made a mental note to have the number changed. Damn Fenwick anyway. He really must have been cracking up at the end.

"I have been thinking," she said without preamble. "I now believe that there are other things I should tell you."

"When?"

"Can you come now?"

"Coffee and cake?"

"As before."

"I'll be there in fifteen minutes." He decided to wait on changing the blue line number and caught a taxi outside the Embassy. It was an overcast day with a steady, cold rain falling. Magda Stanescu's apartment seemed darker than ever. The lights of the brass chandelier cast her face in relief. She looked tired and older. Or was she worried? She was alone except for Franz who arose when he entered, shook hands with a quick, jerky motion, and sat down again on a chair across from the sofa where she indicated with a gesture Scott was to sit beside her. She poured his coffee, remembering that he liked cream and no sugar.

"You have unsettled me some, Mr. Scott, suggesting that my organization might be used by the Communists without my knowledge."

"It's a possibility that I can't overlook in investigating Ralph Fenwick's death. I merely suggested that you shouldn't overlook it either."

"Exactly. It has started a train of thought. An uncomfortable train of thought."

Scott waited.

"Ralph came to Vienna often. You knew that?"

"Once a month for consultation."

"Much more often than that, sometimes several times in a month."

"Why?"

"Sometimes it involved our refugees, but often it involved seeing a girl. I was led to believe that it involved seeing a girl."

"And now you aren't so sure?"

Magda Stanescu grimaced at him. "You see what you suspicious people do to the rest of us? Suspicion, the element of doubt, is like an infection. It spreads rapidly."

"And you have been thinking?"

"I have been thinking that Ralph always posed to me as a ladies' man. So much of his time he accounted for by his love affairs. He never mentioned names. I never inquired. It would have been indiscreet. I am a woman of the world. His private life was his own."

"And now?"

"And now, I say to myself, hypothetically only, you understand, suppose Ralph Fenwick did not have these affairs? What was he doing with his time? If he did not have a woman to see in Vienna, whom he visited often, whom did he visit?"

Franz cleared his throat. "We must not be too quick to lose confidence in Fenwick," he admonished gently. "I saw him on these trips as a waiter. I have observed scores of affairs and rendezvous at the hotel. He had all of the symptoms, gaiety, much laughter, a flushed countenance."

"Did you see the woman?" Scott asked.

Franz spread his hands and shook his head. "He was discreet. No. I did not see the woman."

Magda Stanescu had been staring introspectively into space. "Let us say that it was not a love affair that brought him so often to Vienna, particularly within the last two months when his visits increased. What was it?" She turned to Franz. "Would he have kept contact with any of our refugees? Have any of them stayed in Vienna?"

Franz shook his head, his lips pursed. "I think not. Our refugees wanted to get as far from Eastern Europe as possible, to America and Canada, to build a new life."

Magda Stanescu looked at Scott. "Did you send Ralph to Rome within the last fortnight?"

"No."

"He went to Rome twice, just for a few hours each time."

"He seemed to get around."

"What of the Jewess in Bucharest?" she asked. "At first I thought she might have killed him in a fit of jealousy over the Viennese woman. But if there were no Viennese woman? The Jewess was on the train with him. She would know if he were having a second affair. Courtesans are sensitive to such things." Her eyes raised to his. "You are seeing this woman. You could find out."

"You keep good track of me."

"It's not difficult. You have been quite open about your new liaison."

"She's a cute kid."

Magda Stanescu sniffed. "I suppose that Americanism is appropriate. I can see that she appeals to Americans."

"It isn't all fun and games."

"But isn't it nice to be able to mix business and pleasure?"

"I'm not complaining."

"You could find out from her if Fenwick were seeing another woman here," she repeated.

"Yes. I'll try to do that."

"And Franz and I will try to remember if any of our

refugees are in Vienna or Rome. Through them we might find out what Ralph was doing with his time."

"I am not hopeful," Franz said morosely. "We have not kept a record of our refugees. They were like captive birds that we freed. Once the cage was open they flew away where they wished. We were content just to see them go. I do not like to change things."

"But one of our people has been killed," Magda Stanescu said unhappily. "True, he was one of Mr. Scott's people too and it also may have been only an *affaire du coeur* but, as long as one of the unrefuted possibilities is that he was killed because of his refugee work, I shall be unhappy. Mr. Scott has very cleverly sowed the seeds of doubt in my mind. Now, I have to be sure, Franz, that all is well with our little organization. We can only function if we can trust." She looked at Scott reproachfully. "I can no longer trust."

"I trust. I am sure Ralph Fenwick's death had nothing to do with us," Franz said in a positive voice.

She looked at him affectionately. "Dear, sweet, loyal Franz. That is so like you." She turned to Scott and spoke briskly. "We shall see what we shall see. Meanwhile, I hope you will vigorously investigate the other possibilities in this death."

"Including suicide," Franz added. "We seem to assume only that it was murder."

"Suicide is possible," Scott admitted, "but that answer seems too easy under the circumstances. The police don't think that it was suicide."

Franz threw up his hands in a gesture of resignation. "Very well, Magda dear, we shall assume the worst, but I don't like it. For nearly twenty years we have assumed the best, at least about our own people. It is a mistake to change, but we shall do our utmost, Mr. Scott, to find Fenwick's interest in Vienna or even in Rome. I predict that it will be a woman after all and we shall all feel foolish and you and I, Magda, shall feel a little defiled."

The rain cleared by midday, followed by a brilliant sun in a cloudless blue sky. Scott called for Lani in the Opel and they drove to Hietzing to visit Schonbrunn Palace. They walked with a guide through the seemingly endless corridors and rooms listening to a litany seeking to recreate in the empty, museum-like atmosphere the vitality and purpose of a dead monarchy. They emerged from the chill rooms into the midafternoon warmth of the sunshine with a sense of relief and walked down the graveled paths of the great gardens hand in hand without speaking.

"Was Stein taken care of?" he asked.

She shuddered. "Yes. That is done."

"Still no idea who did it?"

"No. Have you?"

"I just furnished the apartment."

"Let's don't talk about it."

"All right."

"Shall we walk up to the Gloriette?"

"You can't visit Schonbrunn without doing that."

They slowly ascended the slope of the hill on which the graceful, outsized Hapsburg gazebo sat somnolently in the warm sunshine. They sat down on the short clipped lawn below it, overlooking a reflecting pool. The intricate pattern of the eighteenth-century garden lay below them within a framework of snowy-white walks of fine stone and dark green rows of tall cypress trees casting shadows of black across the whiteness. The now verdant green pattern would soon be traced in the reds, blues and yellows of spring flowers nestled within the confines of the tree-lined walks. A soft breeze blew Lani's hair, brushing it from time to time against his cheek as he sat beside her.

"I wish we were just people," she said.

"What would we do differently?"

"Nothing, perhaps. But it would last."

"Nothing lasts."

"I know," she said sadly. "Ardent love affairs don't endure but for ordinary people they change slowly to something else—family, companionship. Sometimes only shared boredom. But they aren't alone."

"There are worse things than being alone."

"I hate it," she said with feeling.

Cupping a match between his hands, he lit a cigarette and handed it to her. She inhaled the cigarette smoke as she watched him light one for himself. "If I came to America and you were just a private citizen, would you make love to me?"

"I'd make love with you anywhere."

"Even with all of those beautiful American girls about?"

"They aren't that beautiful."

"In the magazines and the cinema they seem very beautiful. I look in the mirror and feel very plain."

He leaned over and kissed her lightly on her mouth. "The mirror lies."

She smiled an easy smile that spread slowly across her glowing face until it reached the hazel eyes half hidden by her long, lowered lashes. "Am I as pretty as some American girls, do you think?"

"I think."

She looked at him, pouting. He laughed and took her into his arms. "You are the most beautiful one of all, Lani. You don't need a magic mirror to tell you that."

Lani raised soft lips to his, touching them with a warm lingering kiss. "I love you," she said contentedly. She contemplated the light yellow palace in the distance for a moment. "If we were in America, would you marry me?"

"If I married anyone, I'd marry you."

She gave a faint sigh. "I want to be married, you know. I don't really want to do what I am doing."

He gave her a little, sympathetic hug, but said nothing.

"Tell me," he asked after a moment. "Did Ralph have a mistress in Vienna?"

He felt her stiffen slightly in his arms. "Why do you ask me that?"

"He was coming to Vienna without my knowledge. He also flew to Rome a few times from Vienna, just for the day. The most reasonable explanation for something like that is a woman."

Her voice was low, almost embarrassed. "I don't think he had a woman in Vienna."

"Why?"

She looked at him defiantly. "He had me in Bucharest. He didn't need anyone else."

In spite of himself he was irritated at the blunt frankness of her answer. "I keep forgetting he was your lover," he said, an edge in his voice.

"Do you? Then why did you ask me such a question?"

"I had to know the answer."

"Well, now you know." She looked at Scott. "If he had another woman, I would have known it. You sense these things in bed," she added maliciously.

"You're acting like a cat."

"And you are acting like some sort of procurer. You will do anything for information, won't you? Even make love to a tarnished woman." She struggled to free herself.

Scott held her tightly until she stopped struggling and burst into tears. He kissed her wet cheeks, tasting the salt of her tears on his lips. "I am sorry, Lani, dear. I didn't mean to hurt you. Don't say such wounding things." She sobbed in his arms, crying like a child. After a few minutes she stopped and lay still, letting him stroke her hair.

"We use each other, I know," she said tremulously. "I used you last night and you used me today. Why can't we just love each other?"

"You know why."

"It was such a lovely afternoon."

"Yes."

She sat up and wiped her eyes with a handkerchief. "I am a mess," she said, looking into the mirror of a compact. She carefully made up her face and then smiled at him. "I am sorry, Bob, to act so emotional. It is just that when you asked the question about Ralph I was dreaming of life with you in America. It shattered the dream to bits."

"It's better not to dream."

"I won't do it again."

He helped her to her feet and smiled at her. "I'll tell you when."

"Someday I can dream again?"

"I hope so."

He left Lani in the late afternoon at her apartment, promising to return for an American evening on the town. "We'll see an American movie on *Mariahilferstrasse*," he promised. "And I know a place where we can get a malted milk and a hot dog afterward."

"That is what you do on a date in Indiana?"

"Sure."

"I will love it."

When he returned to the Embassy, there had been a message for him on the blue line. He called the number left in the message. "I want to see you at once," Magda Stanescu said. "I have made a very disquieting discovery. I think I know who Ralph was seeing in Vienna."

"Where should I come?"

She gave him the address of a little bierstube in the Innerstadt off the Graben. He had been waiting about five minutes at a worn wooden table in the rear of the room, a stein of dark beer before him, when she arrived. After she had been served her stein of beer by the waiter she leaned forward. "This has been a black day for me, Mr. Scott, but first, what did you learn from the Jewess?"

"She was very positive that she was the only love in his life."

"It was not vanity?"

"No. I don't think so."

Magda Stanescu nodded. "I sensed that it was not a woman he was seeing the instant you raised the doubt. Before, you see, it made no difference what he did in Vienna or whether or not it was a woman he was seeing. But as soon as I knew it was important that I knew what Ralph was doing in Vienna I also knew that his visits did not involve a woman. A virile man preoccupied with a sexual conquest gives off a certain atmosphere. I, too, am very alive sexually. I can always tell. It interests me and excites me even when I am not the object of it. Ralph did not have this atmosphere about him when he visited Vienna. I realize this now, but I wanted the Jewess to confirm it. Her perceptions would have been even more acute than mine."

"I've heard of female intuition," Scott said dryly. "You make it sound almost like an outsized olfactory sense."

Magda Stanescu sipped her beer. "I believe now that he was in contact with one of our refugees of some years ago, a very distinguished psychiatrist."

"That sounds more innocent than if it had been a woman."

"Ralph had no need for psychiatry."

"You mean the psychiatrist is a front of some kind?"

"I don't know what he is. It was not quite true what I said to you before Franz. I do have some personal records of our refugees. I am ashamed to have him know it because I pretend that they fly away from us free. Actually, I am far too practical for that. I keep essential information so that I can obtain help from them quickly if I need it. The world, this Central European world, is too uncertain not to take these personal precautions. You understand?"

Scott nodded. "A sailor would call it keeping an anchor to leeward. That's in case the main anchor to windward pulls up."

"Exactly. A second chance, yes? We understand each other." She lit a cigarette with a quick, nervous gesture. "In these secret records of mine I find this psychiatrist. He now has a different name than the one we gave him. I now realize also that I can't trace him to his place of origin. His sponsor has disappeared. In other words I can't prove that he is part of our family. He may never have been. He may have been a stranger."

"Who arranged for this man to come West?"

"Franz."

"Franz?"

"That is why we are meeting in a bierstube rather than in my apartment."

"I am sorry." She sighed and waved away his sympathy with a gesture. "A number of my comfortable illusions are in peril today."

"How do you know Ralph saw this man?"

"I can't tell you that. I can say that Ralph saw him in Vienna, in Rome, and perhaps elsewhere. He has an international reputation."

"What is this psychiatrist's name?"

She seemed about to speak and then remained silent.

"I can't do much with this information, Miss Stanescu," Scott spoke softly, "unless you tell me who he is so that I can investigate his background."

"I know that. I should tell you. I fully intended to tell you when I asked you to meet me here. But, now this doubt remains. Perhaps I am being unfair to this man and to Franz and to Ralph. Ralph may have had an entirely innocent reason for visiting this man."

"Such as?"

She shrugged. "I don't know. It was against the rules. I am so worried."

"Then give me the name. I will prove your doubts or put them to rest."

She looked at him bleakly. "You have the resources to learn of this man's past. You can restore my faith in Franz. I must trust those about me. Otherwise, I can't go on with my work."

He nodded.

"Also you can completely destroy my faith in Franz. Where there is a doubt now, you can make it a certainty."

"Yes, I can do that too. It depends where truth lies."

She shivered. "I am afraid, you see? I am not sure I want to know the truth."

"You can't go back now," he said gently.

"Give me more time. I must think."

"There is not much time."

"I must have what there is."

Scott laid some bills on the check. "Will you call me as soon as you have made your decision?"

"Yes." She arose.

"Thank you for the information you have given me."

"It was for my peace of mind."

He took Lani to the American movie and bought her a rather pallid Viennese version of a malted milk and a vivid Viennese version of a hot dog. He then firmly kissed her good night at her door and returned to his apartment on *Josefstaderstrasse*. He was drinking a cup of coffee and looking over some reports when the telephone rang. "Scott," he said tersely.

"Please come to my apartment at once." It was Magda Stanescu's muffled voice. "I will give you the name."

"I'll be there in ten minutes."

He parked around the corner from Magda Stanescu's apartment building and walked in a light spattering of rain to the entrance. High banked clouds and gusts of wind bearing dust and bits of paper along the street indicated that a rainstorm was about to break.

There was no answer when he rang the bell under her apartment number. He pushed the inner door of the lobby. It was ajar so he walked up the stairs to her landing. He pushed the worn brass bell button on the door frame. There was no response. He then noticed that this door also was ajar. A surging sensation of danger flooded over him. His right hand instinctively slipped inside his coat to touch the pistol in the shoulder holster under his left armpit. He pushed open the door and entered the apartment vestibule with a number of reproductions of deer antlers serving as coat hooks on either side of a large, mottled mirror in a heavy carved walnut frame. A clock in the next room struck the half hour with a single stroke. Scott listened intently. There was no other sound. He moved into the living room with its brass chandelier and coffee table. A bottle of scotch and several glasses had been placed upon it. Two lamps of teakwood with heavy embroidered shades bathed the room in a soft glow.

He moved down a short hallway. It led to a butler's pantry and a large old-fashioned kitchen, both lit by ceiling lights, both empty. He returned to the living room. A second hallway opened off the room in the other direction. He walked down it until he came to a bedroom door. It was closed. He slowly turned the handle, hearing the click of the latch as it disengaged. The room was brightly lit by a small crystal chandelier and two table lamps. Magda Stanescu was lying on the floor before a dressing table. Scott moved forward and leaned over her. She had been shot at close range. Powder burns were on her forehead. Blood had run from a wound above her right eye down her cheek to form a pool of blood under it on the carpet. Scott felt for a pulse and lifted one of the eyelids. She was dead. The storm broke outside. Gusts of wind and rain shook the bedroom windows. A creak in the carpeted wooden floor told him that someone was standing behind him. He glanced around. It was Franz regarding him from large dark eyes set in a pale face. Scott rose to his feet and stood facing him.

Franz's eyes dropped to the body. "What has happened?"

"I was about to ask you."

"She is dead."

"Yes."

Franz took his hand out of his coat pocket. It held a gun. "I am afraid, Herr Scott, that you are in deep trouble."

"You think I did it?"

Franz shrugged. "Someone did."

"Yes, someone did."

"It might well have been you."

"Why?"

"Appearances suggest it and I believe in appearances."

Scott glanced down at the body. "She was shot at very short range within the last fifteen minutes by someone she knew. That someone was aware that I was coming here and arranged for me to walk in on this."

Franz slowly shook his head. "No, Herr Scott, it was like this: I appeared on the scene as you were committing the murder. Unfortunately, I was not soon enough to prevent it, but in a fit of outrage I shot you dead on the spot."

"That's the way it was?"

"I fear so, Herr Scott."

Scott looked at him levelly. "Is protecting this psychiatrist really worth all this?"

Franz's smile was wintry. "So she did tell you about the psychiatrist. I am relieved. I hate killing on suppositions."

"What is he? A Russian Spy Master?"

"He is many things, Herr Scott, and well worth the precautions I am taking on his behalf. I am not too concerned about you. Even your own government considers you expendable. I do regret that Magda had to die. We had many years of pleasant association. But however well-meaning, she was a fool. After the first few years following the war her refugee program was a fantasy. Fortunately, I had the opportunity to convert it to contemporary uses. Once you suggested this to her and she began to question the reality of the myth I had provided for her, she had to die. It is better this way. She would not have been happy in the real world as you and I know it."

"You struck me from the first as a humanitarian."

"Tell me, Herr Scott, since the situation allows us to be frank with one another, whom did I kill in your apartment? At the time in the dark I assumed it was you, since he entered the front door using a passkey."

"It was an Israeli agent named Stein."

Franz raised his eyebrows. "A Jew entering an American agent's apartment by stealth? That seems unnecessary since the American governing class is Jewish."

"He was worried about the Arabs, I believe," Scott said coldly.

Franz gave a dry chuckle. "How quixotic. He was, as the Jews would say, a *shlimazel*."

"A born loser."

"Exactly." The storm struck at the windows with renewed fury. Franz's facial muscles became taut. "This is a good night for this business, Herr Scott. The sounds of the storm will mufflle even the small noise from the silencer I am using."

The lights winked once and went out. Scott dived low for Franz's legs as the bullet from the pistol whipped past just above his head. In the darkness he grasped the legs below the knees and spilled Franz over his left shoulder. He turned and fell heavily on the body of the older man and managed to grasp the forearm of his gun hand. It was a poor grip. Franz, in a fury of energy, tore the arm loose. The arms of both men flailed around in the darkness. The pistol discharged again and Scott felt a searing stab of pain in

.93.

his left thigh. He reached out desperately and seized Franz's wrist. Franz kicked Scott in the groin and rolled violently to the right in an effort to break free. The gun discharged again in the darkness. Franz stiffened and became still. Scott continued to lay on top of him, half nauseated from the pain of his wound and the kick in the groin, breathing heavily, holding Franz in an iron grip.

The lights flickered on again. Scott looked at the man beneath him. He was unconscious, his breath coming in brief, ragged flutters. From a wound in his middle chest, a heavy, red bloodstain was spreading. Some of the blood had stained the front of Scott's jacket. While Scott stared into the gray face, the ragged flutters of breath were interrupted by a strangled half cough and stopped. Scott slowly got to his feet and hobbling over to a pink satin slipper chair, sat down. His left trouser leg was torn and scorched. He had a painful flesh wound about three inches long and about one-sixteenth of an inch deep. It could have been worse.

He sat in the chair, surveying the wreckage of the room as he regained his breath. He then got up and critically examined Franz's body and the position of his wound. The pistol was still clutched in the dead man's hand. Appearances suggested that Franz had quarreled with Magda, shot her, and then shot himself. He grinned wryly. Almost the same scene Franz had intended to arrange for him. He liked this casting much better and it would make things easier for the Austrian police when they discovered the bodies . . . no international complications.

He cautiously retraced his steps back through the apartment, carefully wiping all of the doorknobs and furniture he might have touched. Outside in the street the storm had subsided, though heavy streams of water still poured from the eaves and coursed down the gutters. He limped back to the Opel and drove to *Josefstaderstrasse.*

AVVVVVVVVVVVVVVVVVVVVVVVVVVVVVVVA

.9.

A bright shaft of sunlight poured through the newly washed, curtainless windows of the coffeehouse off the *Karntnerring,* bathed Scott's shoulders in a comforting warmth, and spilled onto the morning newspaper which he held before him in a slightly raised position by means of a heavy wooden rod attached to the newspaper's spine. He rolled the newspaper on the rod, reducing its exposed area, until the portion he was reading was in the shadow cast by his body. Absently, he sipped the strong Viennese coffee and milk as he read and munched on a flaky croissant.

Except for his table by the window, the rest of the large public room remained in shadow, its dark walnut paneling and plaster surfaces of muddy yellow absorbing the light from the street, making the light fixtures which burned steadily in the high ceiling a daytime as well as a nighttime necessity. Only three other tables at some distance were occupied in this off hour by customers who had long since finished their coffee and were now absorbed in methodically reading through every newspaper on the racks placed about the room.

Scott shifted in his chair with a wince. The doctor the CIA used in Vienna had dressed his wound that morning without comment. In a week it would heal. This morning it burned like hell.

"Mr. Scott?" a rather thin and high-pitched voice spoke softly beside him. As he looked up from his paper a small, dapper man sat down in a chair drawn from a nearby table. He was not now placed at the other table, nor was he quite at Scott's table, but awkwardly in the aisle between. "May I join you for a moment?"

Scott eyed him without expression. "Sure, go ahead."

The little man hitched his chair toward Scott's table. "Thank you. I hesitate to disturb. You are reading, but I am charged to speak with you and I have discovered there are few opportunities."

"You've been following me around?"

"I've done my best."

Scott finished his coffee and lit a cigarette. "I don't know that I like that."

"You live a most interesting life, Mr. Scott." The words were spoken with a little deprecating smile. "Most interesting. Beautiful ladies . . . I envy you. But all of this is safe with me, Mabruk Mansour." He extracted a slightly soiled card from his coat pocket and pushed it toward Scott as he spoke.

Scott glanced at it. "You are a travel agent?"

Mansour spread his hands. "The card must say something, Mr. Scott. I do not necessarily vouch for its accuracy." His grin revealed several gold fillings.

"What's on your mind?"

"Mr. Scott," Mansour's voice dropped to a near whisper, "Can you visit Venice within the next forty-eight hours? Are you free to leave Vienna?"

Scott leaned back, away from Mansour's intent, out-thrust face, and regarded him through narrowed eyes. "I could. Why should I?"

"You would learn something of great interest about Mr. Fenwick."

"Why don't you tell me now? Why should I go to Italy?"

"I don't have the information about Mr. Fenwick. My principal does and he has charged me to speak to you."

"Who is your principal?"

Mansour moved his chair close to Scott's. His voice became almost inaudible. "Does Farouk Hakim mean anything to you?"

"Yes. It does."

"It is he who would speak to you."

"Why Venice?"

"Hakim is not now in Syria. Since the Six-Day War his position has deteriorated. At the moment, the leader of a pro-American opposition in any Arab country, particularly Syria, is not, shall we say, well placed. He has moved incognito to a place in the Balkans, accessible to Venice. He cannot risk visiting Vienna. I have advised against it."

"Why me?"

"Both of you are anxious to assess the meaning of the death of Mr. Fenwick at the earliest possible time."

Scott looked thoughtfully at the smoke curling up from his cigarette end.

"How do I know that you aren't putting me on?"

"I beg your pardon?"

"What are your bona fides?"

"Alas, I have none, but am I asking too much? A day of your time away from the lovely temptations of Vienna? Have you so much more to learn here in Vienna about Mr. Fenwick? I think not. The Israelis are on you like flies. You will learn nothing." His mouth twisted as if he had bitten on something bitter. "And if you wish the love of Miss Lani Evron, if you can afford this love, I am sure that she will await you here or follow you to Italy if you wish."

"I'm no fool, Mansour," Scott said shortly.

"I hope not, my friend. But I warn you about this woman and her associates."

"Some of her associates are vulnerable, it seems."

A faint smile started in Mansour's dark eyes but he suppressed it before it reached his mouth. "We are all mortal, Allah be praised."

"Were you in on that?"

The voice and expression were bland. "No. I can assure you, no. We do not have the luxury of a public treasury to finance such operations. I am a mere observer. A courier. I lack the funds to be otherwise."

.100.

Scott considered a moment. "O.K. I'll come to Venice. You'll set it up?"

"With pleasure. I will meet you seemingly by chance in the Piazza San Marco at ten in the morning the day after tomorrow. Don't recognize me until I recognize you. I shall have the final details of the rendezvous for you then."

"Will do."

Mansour slid from his chair. "My thanks, Mr. Scott. You are a man of decision and you judge a man by his character . . . not his papers, which we both know can be easily forged. I appreciate that." He glanced casually around the coffeehouse and walked to the door. After several quick, darting glances he stepped into the crowd of passersby moving down the sunlit street and disappeared.

Scott sat in a heavily varnished rattan chair before a small marble-topped cafe table and observed the midmorning activity in Venice's Piazza San Marco. Long shadows lay across the gray paving blocks of the square, which were still wet from an early hour hosing of water. Yet the sun shone with a brilliance equal to the middle of the day on the ornate white facade of a building opposite, hung with a long blue and gold banner announcing an art exhibition. Absent this morning was the murmur of a multitude of inaudible voices which had filled the great square the night before to echo and reecho in a ghostly cadence off the bricks and stones of the ancient masonry surrounding the square. The tables of the cafes were less than one-third filled by a scattering of people absorbed in consuming strong coffee with milk and rolls and in reading their morning newspapers rather than in talking.

Scott buttered a flaky roll as he watched a priest in a long black robe and a wide-brimmed black hat hurry past. A few tables away a group of young American girls were studying maps and guide books and counting small piles of unfamiliar Italian money as they prepared for another day of sightseeing. He felt a sudden surge of regret that he was not in Venice as a tourist. What a wonderful city for fun. What a lovely day to be carefree and uncommitted, to decide what glass factory or basilica to visit. He sighed without realizing it, finished his coffee and lit a cigarette.

He was reading a newspaper when Mansour appeared beside him.

"Mr. Scott! What a pleasure to see you in Venice."

Scott glanced up with an uncertain smile. "Yes, good morning."

"May I sit down? You don't remember me? We met at the opera ball last February."

"Of course. Of course. Please sit down." Scott attempted an expression of dawning recognition.

Mansour pulled up a chair beside him. "Many thanks, I can only stay one moment." His face remained wreathed in a broad smile, but his voice dropped and his dark eyes bore intensely into Scott's.

"At eleven o'clock go to the jetty on the Grand Canal before the doge's palace. Take the gondola with the bright red cockpit. He has his instructions. You understand?"

"Yes."

Mansour's voice rose again. "No, I have had my coffee. I merely noticed you sitting here and I wished to greet you, to take my opportunity." He arose, briefly shook hands, and departed, walking rapidly toward one of the narrow streets opening off the piazza.

Scott resumed reading his newspaper. He glanced at his wristwatch after a few minutes. It was ten twenty. He gestured to a white-jacketed waiter standing among empty tables some distance away, idly sucking air between his teeth and occasionally flipping a white napkin at a table top. When the waiter approached him, he ordered another coffee.

At ten forty-five, he methodically paid his check, folded the newspaper under his arm, and walked slowly to the corner of the piazza where the soft ocher of the brick shaft of the campanile soared skyward, thrusting up beyond the lower silhouettes of the massive buildings that lay in shadow beneath it until the pointed tower, framed in shimmering white, caught the rays of the sun.

Beyond the campanile he studied the Byzantine facade of the church of San Marco until the great clock nearby surmounted by the golden winged lion of Venice prepared to strike the hour. He watched the mechanical figures perform in the little window above the clock's great circular face and then turned casually away to walk the hundred meters to the Palace of the Doges and the Grand Canal.

A freshening breeze was blowing in from the Adriatic across the roadstead before Venice and into the lower reaches of the Grand Canal. It rumpled Scott's hair and brought with it the clean smell of sun and salt and sea, of broad distances and faraway places, of the half-mystical world of promise and carefree gaiety that all men dream lies just below a familiar horizon or beyond a confining breakwater. He walked out on the stone jetty lying between two of the ornate lamps that lined the broad promenade beside the canal. A flight of stone steps discended to the water both to the right and to the left. Lying a few feet off the lower step of the right-hand flight was the long, narrow hull of a black gondola. Its battered cockpit was painted fire-red which accented the worn shabbiness of the black leather cushions on the seats. The gondolier, dressed in black trousers with a black sweater over his white shirt, stood aft on his platform keeping the gondola on station in spite of the roughness of the water, by expert use of his single oar.

Scott walked down the stone staircase until he stood just above a step covered with sea lichen and moss over which the rough water lapped rhythmically.

"You are for hire?" he called to the gondolier.

"Suo nome, signore?"

"Scott."

"*Si, si. Un momento.*" With two or three deft movements of the oar he brought the gondola against the step and held it there.

Scott waited until the boat had risen with the swell and was about to fall, then he stepped onto the gunwale and grasping the metal tubular frame that supported the canvas awning over the cockpit, swung aboard.

Immediately the gondola moved away from the jetty, rolling slightly until the gondolier had it headed into the wind. In five minutes they had moved up the Grand Canal and into calm water. Among the ancient medieval houses that lined the canal, the fresh wind died and the air was filled with the pungent odors of the city.

As they passed a small opening between buildings the gondola swung sharply to the right and entered it. They glided silently over smooth water down a narrow waterway arched by occasional wrought iron pedestrian bridges which served minute cobbled streets winding among the congestion of buildings. In a few minutes they came alongside another gondola which was docked against a narrow walkway parallel to the canal. Its cockpit awning was of deep blue and red striped canvas. Similar canvas drops concealed the interior. As the gondolas touched together, the adjacent canvas drop parted, a man's firm voice spoke, "Join me here, Mr. Scott."

Scott stepped from his gondola to the other and the gondola with the red cockpit moved rapidly away again. In a moment the gondola in which he was now sitting began to move.

In the gloom and closeness of the shrouded cockpit he gazed across at a tall, tanned, athletic-looking man with iron-gray hair. The man smiled and put a forefinger to his lips. After a few minutes Scott could tell from the outside sounds that they had reentered the Grand Canal. His companion leaned forward and extended his hand. "I am Farouk Hakim. Thank you, Mr. Scott, for coming to Venice to see me and for cooperating with our precautions. I think on this gondola in the Grand Canal we can speak safely."

Scott shook the offered hand and smiled briefly. He decided to come immediately to the point. "I understand that you knew Ralph Fenwick."

"Yes. Rather better than I should."

"Why do you say that?"

Hakim spread his hands. "He is dead. One doesn't know why or how. There is little advantage in dealing with a victim. If one could foresee the future one would choose always to do business with the victimizers, not the victims."

"You had Fenwick pegged as a victimizer?"

"He represented the United States, Mr. Scott. That was important to me."

"In what way?"

Hakim's face grew grave. "You know nothing about

this? I was under the impression that Mr. Fen-wick . . ."

"I find," Scott said dryly, "that I didn't know all that Mr. Fenwick did."

"I see," Hakim said slowly, wetting his lips. "I am not entirely surprised. You see, Mr. Scott, I am afraid that I have been indiscreet with Mr. Fenwick. Now that he has proved to be . . . vulnerable, shall we say, I am worried about it."

Scott offered Hakim a cigarette and after lighting it, held the match to his own, waiting for him to continue.

"I am that increasing rarity in the Arab world, Mr. Scott, a pro-United States leader. Perhaps that is too strong. I am, more accurately, an Arab leader who is not anti-United States. In my country the government is run by the Baathists. They are definitely anti-United States. My objective is revolutionary, to depose the Baathists. To succeed, I need outside support. It will not come from Russia; they are satisfied with the Baathists. It will not come from the British; they are reducing their middle-eastern commitments. It will not come from the French; they are playing a different game. That leaves the United States."

Hakim deeply inhaled his cigarette and looked thoughtfully inward for a moment. "I have actively sought that support. I discussed it with Mr. Fenwick in Bucharest. He encouraged me and I told him more of my revolutionary plans than was wise. I am now deeply worried that he did not speak for the United

States, that in fact he may have passed on these plans to the Israelis, or even worse, to my Arab enemies, or, worst of all, to the Russians. They would know how to use it. Already, since the Six-Day war, my political movement is in ruins. In Syria only an anti-United States, pro-Russian policy is possible at the moment. I must wait. But if my plans were revealed, if it were known that I had taken an American agent into my confidence, I would be destroyed as a Syrian political leader. In addition, many lives are at stake."

"I am afraid that in this matter Fenwick did not speak for the United States. He did not report his conversations with you to me and I was his immediate superior."

"I see," Hakim said bleakly. "This is the worst possible truth."

"You are thinking that Fenwick was a double agent?"

Hakim nodded slowly. "It is one possibility. Of course, he may have been an entrepreneur in these matters and have retained my confidences until he could sell them to the highest bidder. In that case the information may have died with him. May Allah will that it is so."

"When he died he was heading West."

Hakim's smile was bitter. "That was his mistake, a bad choice. Who was there to kill him if he had been running East?"

"I have been thinking that you may have killed him."

Hakim spread his hands. "Without a moment's hesitation, Mr. Scott, had I known what I have now learned from you. As it was, I merely had an observer on the train. And think, if I had killed him, would I have come to Venice from the Balkans at some risk merely to arouse your suspicions against me?"

"It wouldn't have been logical."

"I may not be an infallible judge of men, particularly of Americans, Mr. Scott, but I am the most logical of persons in my actions." He raised the curtain and gave a short order to the gondolier. "We shall take you to a jetty convenient to your hotel. I shall return to my vigil in the Balkans. I am at one with my fate, whatever it may be."

The gondola moved smoothly through the water. Hakim threw the partially smoked butt of his American cigarette over the side through a slit in the canvas drop and carefully lit a thin, black oval from his own cigarette case. After inhaling, he sat closely watching the smoke curling up from the glowing end. A faint perfume from the tobacco filled the cockpit. "Tell me, Mr. Scott, did you know Ralph Fenwick frequently visited a psychiatrist?"

"No."

"You should have known this, I think."

"Tell me now."

"His name is Doctor Anton Niesner. He has an office in Rome."

"And in Vienna?"

"That is true. Then you know of him?"

"I've heard the name."

Hakim put the cigarette to his lips. "That is all I know. But it is interesting, is it not? An American agent visiting a psychiatrist? It does not engender confidence. When I first learned of it, I began to worry." He sighed. "I have worried much since."

"Do you think Niesner is a foreign agent?"

"Perhaps."

"Russian?"

"If you require me to guess, Mr. Scott, I would say Israeli, but it is a mere guess based more on my prejudices than on fact."

"You are disarmingly frank."

Hakim laughed softly. "That is why I am frank, Mr. Scott. It *is* disarming." The gondola moved alongside the jetty. He extended his hand.

"I am in your debt, Mr. Scott, you have come a long way and I appreciate your news; though it is not what I had hoped for, it has taught me to keep my own counsel and that is a lesson of great value. I hope that in some way my information has helped you as well."

Scott smiled. "It explains one passenger on the train and makes me a little more certain that Fenwick had feet of clay."

"He was a most dangerous man to know," Hakim murmured. "A most dangerous man."

AAAAAAAAAAAAAAAAAAAAAAAAAAAAAA

.10.

It was only a fortnight past the equinox, but Rome was already unseasonably warm. A midday sun beat down from a cloudless blue sky upon the awnings that extended over the uneven sidewalk before the small cafe off the Via del Corso, casting the small steel-banded circular tables with their green tubular steel legs into a welcome shadow.

Scott trudged up the small incline to the cafe looking hot and tired in his plaid cotton sport shirt, an orange guidebook protruding from a pocket and a camera slung over one shoulder. He dropped into a chair and smiled at the white-jacketed waiter who instantly appeared.

"I'll have a campari."

"*Si, signore.* At once." The waiter returned with the drink and placed it before Scott with a small paper napkin. "You have seen the Trevi Fountain? It is nearby."

"Yes," Scott patted the camera case. "I took several pictures."

"Did you throw in the coins for good luck?"

"I did that too."

The waiter shrugged. "The Americans must desperately need good luck. They give the fountains most of the money they receive, then follows the Germans and the British. The French give very little and we Italians even less. We must be very lucky already."

Scott laughed. "I think you are. This is a beautiful city. Millions come to see it each year."

"To visit, it is beautiful. Living here is not so easy." The waiter gave a nearby table a mournful swipe with his towel and disappeared inside the cafe.

Scott sipped his campari and glanced at his watch. It was twelve thirty. At twelve forty, Jim Boad, Scott's CIA opposite number in Rome, dropped down in a chair beside him. "Hi."

Scott continued to gaze at his guidebook, which he had open on the table before him. "You're late," he said casually. "We'll never get any sightseeing done at this rate."

Boad yawned. "I start slowly on this tourist bit. What's that?" he indicated Scott's drink.

"Campari."

"Bring me one of those," he said to the waiter, who had appeared beside him. When they were alone, he lowered his voice. "This business or pleasure, Bob?"

"Business."

"I was afraid of that."

"Let's rent a car and I'll fill you in."

"We can use mine."

"No. We'll rent one at random. I'll feel safer that way."

"It's like that, huh?"

.112.

"Yes. It's like that."

They rented a small red Fiat and drove out of the crowded city, across a narrow bridge spanning the Tiber, and onto the highway lined with wispy pine trees leading to Ostia and the Tyrrhenian Sea. As the traffic thinned, Jim Boad glanced at Scott from the driver's seat. "What's up?"

Scott lit a cigarette and slowly put the match packet back into his trousers pocket before replying. "You knew Fenwick got it?"

"Yes, I heard. Too bad. You working on it?"

"Yes."

"What's the Rome angle? I thought Fenwick was a Balkan operator."

"He was. I was his control out of Vienna. Since he died a rather interesting thing has happened. I've been sought out by a number of people each with a story about Fenwick. I'm convinced of one thing. Fenwick led a busy life."

"A double agent?"

"Maybe. At any rate he seems to have left a lot of loose ends about."

Boad was silent, displaying a professional lack of curiosity about espionage details outside his own assignment.

"One of the loose ends is in Rome. Have you ever heard of a Doctor Anton Niesner?"

Boad drove onward for a minute or two, his brows knitted. "Niesner? No. I don't think so. That's a German name, isn't it?" He moved left and passed a slow-moving truck.

"Viennese."

Board shook his head. "No. I've never heard of him."

"I've been informed that he had frequent contact with Fenwick in Vienna, and less frequently in Rome. The implication is that Niesner is a foreign agent, probably Russian."

Board whistled. "This contact was outside Fenwick's operating instructions?"

"Altogether. I knew nothing about these contacts, if they occurred."

"How reliable are your informants?"

"I don't know, but I think we should check Niesner out."

"Will do. You say he's a doctor?"

"A psychiatrist."

"Maybe Fenwick needed a head shrinker—professionally, that is. This is a pretty tough racket we're in."

Scott gave a hard, short laugh. "We need a psychiatrist before we get in, not after."

"How long will you be in town?"

"As long as it takes."

"Business must be slow in Vienna."

"This is business. Remember?"

Board grinned thinly. "I'll see you get the season rates."

Scott returned to the Hotel Excelsior after leaving

Boad and stretched out on the coverlet of his bed to read a paperback book. He soon fell asleep and awoke after darkness had fallen, feeling cold and stiff. He spent ten minutes under a hot shower, dressed in a blue serge suit with a white shirt and a subdued tie and went down the street to the Ambasciatori Bar. He took a seat on a leather-cushioned bench that ran along a wood-paneled wall behind a series of small tables for two and ordered a dry martini. For the first time in several days he felt relaxed and at ease. Rome did this to him. The city was so old, so enduring, that it minimized the cares of the moment and promised that life was full and rich and would continue. Rome had none of the bittersweet sadness of Vienna, where nightfall often suggested loneliness and nostalgia for better times. Rome, at sundown, promised love, music, and excitement. He sipped the martini; very dry, very cold, just right, as a matter of fact. He began to hum a tune from the annual Blackfriar's review of his college days.

"What is that captivating little tune, *neshomeleh*?"

Scott looked up at the sound of the familiar voice. Lani Evron stood smiling down at him. She was wearing a simple dress of rose-colored flannel and had a small matching flower tucked into her heavy hair over one ear.

"It's the hit song from my college review, 'Love is for Everybody.'"

Lani's mouth curved in a half smile. "I like the

title." Her manner was faintly diffident. "May I sit down, or are you waiting for someone?"

Scott scrambled to his feet. "I'm sorry. You surprised me. I know now that I was waiting for you."

"Is that a martini?"

"Yes. A good one, too. I found an unpatriotic bartender who doesn't push the vermouth."

"That's what I shall have." She let him light her cigarette and looked at him from under lowered lashes. "Are you glad to see me?"

"Sure. You are living proof that spying can be fun."

"I think you are making fun of me."

"Not really," he smiled. "I'm just happy to see you."

"I followed you," she said artlessly. "You know, 'whither thou goest, I will go.' "

"That was love."

She looked at him over the rim of her glass as she sipped her martini. "Exactly."

"Have you had dinner?"

"No."

"Where would you like to go?"

"Somewhere with dancing and a quiet table where we can talk."

The restaurant was warm and intimate with walls of wine-red damask and dimly lit crystal and gold chandeliers. An orchestra played from a small raised stage before a tiny dance floor at a sufficient distance from

.116.

their table so that the music provided only a background for conversation.

They danced between courses, Lani's lithesome body close to him, her soft cheek and scented hair brushing his. Over coffee she took his hand and pressed it between both of hers. "This is a lovely evening, darling. I promise you it is an end in itself."

"No body in my hotel room when I get back?"

A shadow crossed her face and she withdrew her hands from his. "That was unnecessary," she said in a hurt voice. "I knew the 'body' as you call it. It was not a game."

"I'm sorry, but we are both here on duty. Let's not forget it."

She looked at him from the corner of her eyes. "You are afraid that I will soften you up, Robert Scott. That is why you are so hard. You feel for me and that makes you afraid."

He nodded. "I feel for you and that makes me afraid. Yes ma'am."

"I am on your side. I can help you."

"Then start helping," he said dryly. "So far it's only been fun and games."

She let him hold a match flame to her cigarette, guiding his hand with one of hers as he did so. She looked at him over the flame after she had lighted the cigarette and removed it from her lips with her free hand. "I shall help you then. You should not trust your James Boad."

He withdrew his hand and deliberately blew out the match. "Why not?"

"He has begun to file false reports about Israel."

"Doesn't everybody?"

She turned to him earnestly and spoke in a low, intense voice, "Don't you see, Bob? Both your CIA man in Bucharest and your CIA man in Rome have been bribed by the Arabs!"

"Not necessarily."

"How can you doubt it?"

"The reports may be true," he said calmly.

She made an impatient gesture with her right hand, the glow of her cigarette tracing a little arc in the dim light. "All right. That is one possibility. But the reports are not true if they accuse Israel of developing secret war weapons without informing the United States and that is what both Fenwick's and Boad's reports say." She leaned toward him. "Can't you see, Bob? Israel can't afford to offend the United States. Our very life as a nation depends upon your support."

"O.K. Let's say that the reports are untrue. That doesn't mean that the Arabs are behind it."

"Who else, but Egypt?" she said bitterly.

"Russia."

"Of course, Russia," she said indifferently.

"You don't believe that?"

"No. You Americans have an obsession about Russia and the Communists. Everything that happens, you accuse the Russians."

"And you Israelis accuse the Arabs."

She looked up at him and smiled. "All right, Bob. Let us say it is the Russians, what then?"

"Have you ever heard of Dr. Anton Niesner?"

She gazed at him wordlessly and nodded.

"In what connection?"

She took out her purse and after looking through it carefully, took out a business card and handed it to him. He held it under the candlelight. It was the card of Dr. Anton Niesner with a Rome office address and telephone number on it. On the back, an hour and date were written in green ink. "You have an appointment with him?" Scott asked incredulously.

"Yes. Tomorrow."

"Why?"

"You won't believe me, darling, I am sure. Your CIA man in Rome, Mr. James Boad, visits him regularly as a patient. I have been asked to visit the doctor and make a report on the physical layout of his office. We may burgle it."

Scott stared at her.

"You don't believe me, you see. Also, you won't believe me when I tell you that Ralph Fenwick used this same psychiatrist in Vienna and sometimes in Rome."

Scott silently poured coffee from a small silver pot. He sipped his slowly before speaking. "Maybe I can believe you. What do you think this means?"

"At the very least, it means you Americans have had two mentally unstable agents," she said lightly.

"Do you think Niesner uses psychiatry as a cover?"

"I think so, yes."

"You think he is an Arab agent?"

"We strongly suspect it."

"There's another possibility."

"Yes?"

"That he is an Israeli agent."

Her sudden peal of laughter rang out in the restaurant. As other diners turned toward them curiously, she put her hand over her mouth. "I'm sorry, Bob, but really, you are quite amusing."

"Fenwick and Boad could both be Israeli double agents," Scott persisted. "Niesner could be their contact."

"If so, why would I accuse Boad and create your suspicions?"

He grinned. "You may be an Arab double agent."

She laughed and leaned over and kissed him on the cheek. "Now you are being silly!"

They arose from the table and danced to several orchestra selections. When they returned to their table he looked at her earnestly. "Lani, let's cooperate on this Niesner thing."

"I think we can," she said slowly. "We both want to know the connection between Dr. Niesner, Fenwick and Boad."

"When is your appointment?"

"At five P.M. It just precedes Boad's. I arranged it that way. We know Boad's routine of appointments.

He visits Dr. Niesner every other day at six in the evening."

"After office hours?"

"More or less. He has a long session with the doctor —sometimes as much as three hours."

Scott lit their cigarettes and thoughtfully blew out the match. "This should be very interesting."

She wrinkled her nose at him. "And in good company."

"And in good company," Scott agreed, grinning.

She put a hand over his. "This means that you believe me, that you trust me."

He shook his head. "You know that I can't really do either, but perhaps I am beginning to believe that we are on the same side."

She smiled, a broad, artless smile that suddenly revealed to him what she must have been like as a young girl. "It's the same thing, you know, darling. Belief, trust, and self-interest, any of the old civilizations will tell you that."

.11.

Scott telephoned Boad the next morning. "Can I see you in your office about five fifteen?"

"Five fifteen? Can't we make it earlier? I have an outside appointment about six."

"Sorry. That's the way the day works out. I may be heading north tomorrow. How about dinner together, say eight o'clock?"

"No, the evening is taken. Well, if today's your last day in Rome, make it five fifteen or earlier if you can."

Was there a note of relief in Boad's voice? Scott wondered as he hung up the telephone. He stared thoughtfully in front of him for a moment. Take it easy. Don't prejudge Boad. Boad said he had never heard of Niesner. Lani said he was one of Niesner's patients. He'd know the answer at six P.M. Scratch one agent or one girl friend. Girl friend? That's what he was thinking. What's more, he knew he hoped Lani was right. Was that sound judgment or was he getting business confused with pleasure? He forced himself to remember that Lani Evron had been on the train with Fenwick. She was an Israeli agent, not an out-of-luck dancer. He shouldn't, couldn't trust her. He glowered. Damn it. His blood raced when he thought of her. He had to cool off. Remain detached. Woman bait was the oldest come-on in the business. He deliberately developed a negative view of Lani during a cold shower and spent a miserable day.

Shortly after five, leaving a taxi waiting around the corner on Via Sallustiana, he entered the courtyard of the Palazzo Margherita which housed the American Embassy behind its rococo facade and took an elevator to an upper floor. Boad had a small cubicle for an office under the eaves.

"It's probably where the coachmen slept," Boad observed sourly, referring to the earlier days when the building was the home of one of Rome's princely families.

Scott glanced out of the small window behind Boad's desk. "Nice view."

Boad shrugged. "I guess so. I'd rather not have a window if the air conditioning worked. There's a hell of a lot of noise from Via Veneto."

Scott sat down in a chair uninvited.

When he did not move or speak, Boad sat on the edge of the desk and nervously swung one leg back and forth. "What can I do you for?"

"You think we can talk safely here or is it bugged?"

Boad hunched his shoulders. "We were clean last week and we make a periodic check, but with all these new electronic devices, who in hell knows? Better you don't mention names, then we know we're safe."

"O.K. Did you check out the name I gave you?"

"Tried to. Nothing turned up yet."

"He's in the telephone book, isn't he?"

"Sure. You know that. There is such a person. I assume you want to know if there's something unusual about him."

"Right."

Boad glanced at his wristwatch. "I have to run along soon, old man, I'll keep in touch. As soon as I have something, you will have it."

Scott leaned back in his chair. "You have plenty of time," he said easily. "I've found out that he's pretty prominent. Funny you never heard of him."

"This is a big town, Bob. There are millions of people in it I've never heard about." He wiped his forehead with his pocket handkerchief. "It's stuffy as hell in here. They never turn on the air conditioning until we peasants are damned near sun-fried. I suppose they save a hundred bucks a year that way."

"Cigarette?" Scott held out a package.

"No," Boad looked at his wristwatch again. "Really, Scott, I've got to blow. I can't be late for this appointment. Traffic is hell at this hour."

"I'll wind it up in a minute. After all, I'm leaving town tomorrow. You're still tied up tonight?"

"Yes."

"Too bad. I hate to rush things."

Boad stood up and reached for his hat. He was perspiring freely. "Sorry to be rude, Scott," he said briskly, "I warned you that I had very little time."

.125.

Scott stood between Boad and the door. "What is it, Jim, a girl friend? You must have it bad."

"Don't be an ass. Let me by."

"Just a second. I think we should have some understanding about when we get in touch."

"I told you, damn it," Boad's voice rose. "I'll call you when I know something. Now will you get the hell out of my way?"

Scott stood gazing at Boad calmly for a moment, noting his flushed damp face and his frantic eyes. He then stood aside without a word.

Boad pushed by him. "Sorry, old man," he mumbled as he wrenched open the door into the passageway. "Terribly sorry. I'll explain later."

Scott waited ten seconds and then hurriedly pushed out his cigarette and followed Boad. He gave the taxi driver Niesner's address in a residential neighborhood of new high-rising apartment buildings beyond the Borghese Gardens and promised an extra tip for speed. Boad had to get his car out of the Embassy parking lot several hundred meters away so it should be possible to arrive in Niesner's neighborhood minutes before him.

The taxi left Scott on a corner a few doors away from the apartment building in which Niesner had his tenth-floor office. It was a slim shaft of cement and glass rising ten stories from the narrow street without a setback. Two small stores occupied the ground floor on either side of a minute marble lobby.

Scott walked into a tobacco shop across the street

and bought a package of cigarettes. He stood well back from the street window and opened the packet, watching the entrance of the apartment building. He felt both a surge of exhilaration and of disappointment when he saw Jim Boad swing a green, dusty Volkswagen into the No Parking space before the building and rush inside. It was five minutes past six.

A few minutes later, Lani Evron emerged from the building and walked slowly toward the nearby corner. She was standing by a small red Fiat roadster inspecting her makeup as Scott approached her. She smiled at him, handed him the ignition keys, and slid into the black leather passenger's seat as he held the door open for her. He did not speak until they were several blocks away.

"Well, you were right."

"Yes. Only you did not believe that."

"I had to be sure."

"Of course."

"I tried to delay him at the Embassy. He was in a dither to get to his appointment. At the end, he nearly walked right over me."

"I saw him when he arrived," she said. "He seemed distraught at being late, almost frightened."

"What is the doctor like?"

"He pretends to be very Viennese, but I think that he is German. The courtliness, the twinkle, the smile, they do not seem real. What seems real is a stern, no-

.127.

nonsense atmosphere of authority when he gets down to business."

"A disciple of Freud?"

"He would not go so far. He would remember that Freud was, after all, a Jew."

"You didn't like him."

She shivered. "I was afraid of him. Of course, as a Jew, that kind of German creates a certain atmosphere for me. I felt like the bird being watched by a belled cat."

"Let's hope he's belled."

"Also, Bob, I don't think that I fooled him. Not even for one moment."

"Do you think he knows who you are?"

"No. I think he only sensed that I did not have the attitude of a patient. At one point he hinted that I might be a newspaper reporter."

Scott laughed.

"I was late because I wanted my appointment to overlap Boad's so that I could get an impression of his relationship to the doctor. That meant that I had to delay at the end, because he wanted to get rid of me. I think he was becoming suspicious so at the last I even flirted with him." She gave a mock sigh. "The things one must do!"

"What was the treatment?"

"Talk. Tell me about yourself. I had to make it all up of course. He could tell that it wasn't the stream of consciousness or whatever they call it."

"Do you have another appointment?"

"No. He assured me that I had no problems."

"What was his attitude toward Boad?"

"Familiar." She glanced at him. "Almost proprietary."

Scott didn't respond and drove silently for a few blocks.

"I am sorry, Bob. I know he is your friend."

"No. We aren't friends. We just are in the same business." He paused. "I don't know what this means."

"You have a man tailing Boad?" he asked after an interval.

"Yes."

"Will you be in touch with him tonight?"

"Yes. At nine o'clock we have a telephone contact, or every half hour thereafter if either of us is delayed."

"I'd like to know when Boad gets home. I'm going to confront him with this Niesner thing."

"The direct American approach."

"It seems called for. A crooked line isn't always the only way between points. A young civilization can teach you that."

She laughed. "Now you are being sensitive. But I agree with you!"

"Good. Because you are such an honest, straightforward, frank girl, I'm going to take you to dinner."

"You are making fun of me again," she said.

"No, my darling. I am not making fun of you." He

grinned and put an arm around her drawing her toward him.

"Can you manage Roman traffic with one hand?" she asked, looking up at him from shadowed dark eyes.

"Yes, but I was just thinking."

"What?"

"I don't like bucket seats."

"But," she whispered. "We aren't going to spend the night in the car."

She made the telephone call at nine o'clock from an instrument brought to their table at the restaurant. There was no answer at nine, nine thirty, or ten. Her eyes sought Scott's. "I am sorry. There must be a complication."

He laid some lire notes on the check before him. "I'll take you to your hotel and wait for Boad at his apartment. He will show up sooner or later."

He drove the open car through the scented spring air of the Borghese Gardens, under the ancient red brick arch of Puerta Pinciana, and swung in an illegal arc to the curbside of the busy entrance of Hotel Flora at the head of Via Veneto.

"Keep the car," she said. "I'll wait for you here."

"It might be late."

"No matter." She kissed him lightly on the mouth and lithely slid from the low-slung automobile.

Boad's apartment was in a great warren of a building rising on one side of a street which twisted away from the Pantheon toward Corso Vittorio Emanuele.

.130.

Scott pressed the worn button in a tarnished brass plate before Boad's name, but there was no response. He was leaning against the exterior of the building lighting a cigarette when an ancient taxicab wheezed up the slight incline and discharged a passenger. It was Boad.

"Hello, Jim," Scott said casually.

Boad started, then grinned. "Christ, I must be getting jumpy. What in hell are you doing here, Bobby Scott?"

"I'd like to talk with you."

"Why not? Why not, I say? Come on up, I'll give you a drink." They entered the musty interior of the building and walked down a broad, badly lit hallway to an old-fashioned lift with a wrought iron gate across an open car. Boad hummed a tuneless air as they ascended, but they did not speak until they were in his over-furnished two-room apartment. Boad walked into the small kitchen and emerged with a bottle of scotch, ice, and two glasses. "Straight or with water?"

"Over ice."

"Right." He handed Scott his drink in a chipped sea-green tumbler and dropped into a chair with his own. He extended his legs and leaned his head on the back cushion. "Jesus, I'm tired. Mrs. Boad's Jimmy has had a busy day."

"Why did you tell me that you didn't know Dr. Niesner?" Scott asked in a casual tone.

.131.

Boad gazed at him from under half-closed eyelids. "Did I say that?"

"You did."

"Well, old man, I'm sorry. You threw the name at me, out of the blue, so to speak. All of these wop names sound alike."

"It's a German name."

"Yes. It is, isn't it?" Boad giggled.

"You went to him tonight. I'm told you visit him several times a week."

Boad waved a deprecatory hand accompanied by a facial grimace, but he did not speak.

"Well?"

"Well, what?"

"Why didn't you tell me you knew Niesner?"

"Well, hell. In this business you don't spill everything you know."

"You don't hold out on members of your own team."

"I would have told you, eventually." Boad downed his drink.

"What is your connection with Niesner?"

"I go to him as a patient."

"A patient?"

"Sure, he's a doctor isn't he? A head shrinker? Well, my head needs shrinking. I think yours does too, Bobby Scott; do you a world of good." He giggled again and got up to refill their glasses.

"You act like you have a high on."

.132.

"No. I'm always like this after a treatment. Great stuff. Amazing how the tensions subside."

"Why didn't you tell me about Niesner?" Scott repeated.

Boad took a swallow of whiskey. "Well, you know, Scott, you don't like to spread it about that you're visiting a head shrinker. People get the wrong idea, like thinking you're off your rocker. This guy is a doctor, like any other doctor. It's just that it's a new science and because it's new, most people have a medieval attitude toward it."

"Why did you need psychiatric help?"

"Tensions. You know, this is a pressure job. I had to find some relief."

"Why Niesner?"

"I don't know," Boad said vaguely. "He's one of the best in the business."

"Who recommended him?"

"I don't remember. Maybe I looked him up in the yellow pages."

"I told you Niesner may have known Fenwick."

"Fenwick? Oh, yeah. The guy that got it." Boad yawned hugely. "Boy, I've got to get some shut-eye."

"I also told you that Niesner may be a Russian agent."

Boad laughed and leaned forward in his chair kneading his close-cropped hair with both hands. "Damn it. Now I'm getting a headache again."

"Again?"

.133.

"That's one of the reasons I go to Niesner. Tension headaches."

"You don't believe Niesner can be a Russian agent?" Scott persisted.

"Hell, no! He's got a daily list of patients a mile long. When would he find the time to be a Russian agent? This practice of his is the real thing, Scott. It's no cover. He's a damned good doctor. Done me a world of good." He rubbed his eyes and stared in front of him.

"What kind of treatments do you have?"

"Couch sessions mostly. I talk and he takes notes, that kind of stuff. Lately he's been trying hypnosis to help the headaches."

"Hypnosis? In your job you submit to hypnosis?"

"What do you mean, 'submit'? This is medical treatment by a trained doctor."

"I say it's dangerous."

"Oh, hell," Boad said irritably. "You don't know a damn thing about it, Scott. It isn't a vaudeville act on a stage. This has a medical purpose. So far as I remember I never say anything. The whole bit is directed toward my subconscious."

"So far as you remember."

Boad sat still staring morosely in front of him.

"Jim. Do you really know what you're doing?"

"Yes."

There was a long silence. Scott watched Boad slowly

become more subdued. He rubbed his eyes and loosened his shirt collar. He had a fit of coughing and rubbed his chest through his open shirt front. Rising from his chair, he walked out into the kitchen and drank a glass of water. When he reentered the room he walked over to the window and stared into the street. Two or three times he pulled the extended fingers of both hands down from his temples and across his cheeks, leaving faint red marks where the nails had been drawn across the skin.

"I'll shove off, Jim," Scott said at last in a low voice.

Boad turned around from the window. "Thanks for coming by, old man. Sorry to run you off. I badly need a night's sleep."

"I'll see you tomorrow."

"You're staying on?"

"For a day or so."

Boad nodded. "Keep in touch, old man. Where are you staying?"

"The Excelsior."

"Right." Boad hesitated. "Bob?"

"Yes."

"Nothing. I guess. Just keep in touch, will you?"

"Sure."

Boad moved with him toward the hallway door. "You can find your way out, old man?"

"Yes."

"Good. I'll just turn in. I am worn out, absolutely

bushed." He looked at Scott with haggard eyes. "I hope to God I can sleep. Bad dreams, you know. Very bad dreams." He patted Scott on the back as he closed the door behind him.

.12.

Scott and Lani Evron walked down Via Veneto from the Hotel Flora hand-in-hand at midmorning and had breakfast together under the bright awnings of Doney's sidewalk cafe. Ordering café au lait, croissants, and large glasses of fresh orange juice, they sat smiling at one another, ignoring the steady stream of pedestrian traffic that flowed down the sidewalk between the row of tables under the awnings and the other row at the sidewalk edge. They touched one another frequently, using any necessary or contrived movement of their hands or bodies as an excuse to renew the physical intimacy of the night before, but they talked very little until they had hungrily eaten their breakfast and were smoking cigarettes over a second cup of coffee.

"It's a beautiful, warm day," she said, closing her eyes and lifting her head to feel the sun's rays which stole through a gap between two awnings to fall on her face.

"Yes. It's a good day for a drive into the country."

"Do you think so? I would love that."

"You have a lovely smooth skin," he said, gazing at her.

She smiled without opening her eyes or speaking.

He reached out and touched her cheek. She turned her face enough to kiss the palm of his hand. *"Liebling,"* she murmured.

The sun's rays shifted and slowly placed her in the awning's shadow again. She opened her eyes and looked at him. "Did you find Boad last night? I was so shamefully lustful I forgot to ask."

"Yes. I talked with him at his apartment. He admits that he sees Niesner frequently as a patient. Nothing more.'"

"Do you believe him?"

"No."

"Why not?"

"He did not act . . . normal."

"Perhaps that is why he is a patient."

"Perhaps." He was silent a moment. "I'll give him a day or so. He may come to me."

"If he doesn't?"

"I'll have him transferred back to the States."

"You have such influence?"

"In a case like this, the facts speak for themselves."

She looked at him inquiringly.

"Two American agents with presumed contacts with Niesner behave strangely," he added.

Her brows drew together. "We have not yet heard from our man who was shadowing Boad."

"No report?"

"None. Neither to me nor to others."

He sipped his coffee and looked thoughtful.

She put a hand lightly over his. "Let's take a holi-day, Bob. There's no need to sit here and brood. Let's go up to Tivoli."

He smiled. "Why not? It's a waiting game."

They drove out from Rome through the spring countryside in the red Fiat convertible. Lani leaned back with her head against the warm leather seat and let the soft scented air blow through her loosened hair. "This is lovely," she murmured.

Scott glanced over at her with smiling eyes and then turned back to concentrate on the road as it wound through greening fields, orchards of flowering almond and fruit trees, and crowded villages bisected by the road which, restricted in size, ran headlong over their one paved street.

They climbed from the Roman plain into the Sabine Hills toward the imperial country seat of the Caesars. By the time they had parked, the sun had climbed to its zenith in a clear blue sky and the day was almost hot.

"Perhaps we should have gone to the ocean," Scott said using a handkerchief on his damp brow.

Lani put an arm lightly through his. "It will be cooler in the garden."

They walked into the ancient house on the brow of the hill. It was still cold and damp from winter. The warmth of spring had not yet penetrated its thick masonry walls. They did not stay long in the dead atmosphere of the past but walked into the gardens bursting with the life and scents of a contemporary surge of life. Everywhere among the flowers, trees, and shrubs was the sound of cascading water diverted centuries before from a river to flow endlessly with the force of gravity through scores of fountains arranged down the hillside in terraces. Crystal water flashed and sparkled among hanging green bows and vines, spilled over walls in satin sheets, thrust into the air in elaborate patterns to fall in mosaic paved receptacles in clouds of mist radiating rainbow colors in the sunlight, finally emerging through openings in intricately designed figures ranging from the sublime to the grotesque to flow along stone channels heavy with moss and lichen before plunging to the next terrace level where it emerged in new patterns and designs against different backgrounds of light and scale.

They spent over an hour among the fountains of Tivoli, silent, relaxed, insulated by their enjoyment of each other's company, and then went to a nearby restaurant for a late lunch.

She idly traced a pattern on a pastel-colored tablecloth with a short, neatly trimmed fingernail. "Where were you born, Bob?"

"In a little town in Indiana, Valparaiso."

"That is Spanish. Is it really a valley of paradise?"

He laughed. "We like it, but even the Chamber of Commerce doesn't claim that. It was named for a sea battle off the coast of Chile near Valparaiso. That's no valley of paradise either."

She smiled wistfully. "I think there is no valley of paradise."

"Nor a land of milk and honey?"

She shook her head. "No. There's no land of milk and honey either. Certainly not in Israel."

"Were you born there?"

"Yes. I am a *sabra*, a native-born. We are supposed to be tough on the outside and sweet on the inside."

"I think you are."

"We do what we have to do to survive. My parents survived the Nazis in Poland and survived the effort to get to Israel so that I might be born in a free country. I have not had to do so much, thanks to God."

"Survival comes first," he murmured. "Everything else follows."

"I suppose life was much different in America?"

"We don't think of our problems in terms of survival. We have forgotten the frontier and take survival for granted."

"I don't think you can do that."

"No. But when one is reared in the middle of the North American continent, it is easy to take survival for granted and even to disbelieve in human mortality until personal experience proves it."

She looked into his eyes. "You have had that experience. Haven't you?"

"I fought in Vietnam," he said simply.

"So, we both have learned. The little *sabra* from Israel grows up knowing that for centuries her people

.141.

have existed almost on sufferance in a hostile world and that her own small country, hard and beautiful, harsh and bountiful, exists in a sea of hostile Arab nations. The boy from mid-America grows up believing in a kind of inherited immortality until he moves into the outside world." She smiled at him fondly. "I think my upbringing is less cruel, darling. I had no illusions to lose."

"We have to have some beliefs. I have a few that keep me going in rough times. 'People are more important than systems. Life is fun. If we don't live in a paradise, neither do we live in a jungle.' They may be illusions, but I don't think so."

"Why are you a spy, Bob?"

He winced involuntarily and then grinned good-naturedly. "I like the company."

She laughed gaily. "So do I." And their talk veered away from serious things to remembered trivia from their past lives that reminded them of the common human experience and brought them closer together.

They parted for a few hours on their return to Rome, but arranged to attend a concert together in the ruins of a basilica in the Forum and to have supper afterward. Scott went to his hotel room, stripped down and stepped into the shower. As he turned off the water and stepped onto the bath mat, the telephone gave a long peal. He wrapped a bath towel around him and padded in his bare feet to the telephone table by his bed, leaving wet footprints behind him. "Scott."

"Where in hell you been?" The irritated voice of Jim Boad asked.

"I've been out in the country."

"This is a hell of a time to do that."

"What's on your mind, Jim?" Scott asked evenly.

"The telephone rang seven times before you answered it." The tone was querulous.

"I was in the shower."

"Can I come up? I'm in the lobby. I've got to see you, Scott."

"O.K. Come on up. Room 208."

"208. Right." The line went dead with a sharp crackle as Boad hung up.

Scott had just time to slip into a shirt and a pair of slacks when a series of sharp raps reverberated on the door panel.

"Jesus," Boad said as he came in the door. "I thought I'd never find you."

Scott looked at Boad's haggard and drawn face and poured three fingers of scotch into a drinking glass and handed it to him. "Take it easy, chum. Sit down."

Scott sat on the edge of his bed and lit a cigarette as Boad dropped onto a nearby straight chair and drained the glass.

"Good. I needed that, thanks," Boad said glancing at him. His eyes dropped to the floor and he began to turn the glass between his hands. Twice he looked as if he would speak, but he did not and Scott patiently waited.

"Bob," Boad said at last in a muffled voice. "I think I've killed a man." He looked at Scott with an involuntary giggle and then his face contorted in a nervous grimace. He reached for the scotch bottle and tipped it into his glass with shaking hands.

"In the line of duty?" Scott asked calmly.

Boad shook his head vaguely. "No. At least I don't think so. I don't really remember. That's the hell of it, Bob." He looked at him with anguished eyes. "That's the hell of it," he emphasized the word as his voice trailed off in a husky whisper.

"It's probably just your imagination."

"I don't think so," Boad said hollowly. "I keep remembering it in snatches like a flash now and then. I see this guy, see? I'm in the dark somewhere, maybe it's a park. I surprise him, see? I hate his guts. Jesus, how I hate his guts. But who is he, see? Who in hell is he, Scott? Where did it happen? When did it happen?" His eyes dropped to his hands. "I strangled him, Scott. I strangled him." He flexed his fingers back and forth and then with a dry sob buried his face in his hands.

"We have to kill in this business, Jim. It wouldn't be the first time."

"It's not that, don't you see? It's that I can't remember how it was or if it was. And why? Why in hell did I do it? Who was this guy? Have I become a casual killer who doesn't even remember, for God's sake?

Maybe I ought to be committed, Scott. Maybe I ought to be put away."

"Was this what Niesner was treating you for?"

A crafty look came over Boad's face. "Niesner? Who told you about Niesner?"

"We've talked about Niesner before, Boad. I know all about it."

"Yes. I remember that." Boad nodded solemnly two or three times. "No. Niesner has nothing to do with this. I'm sure of that."

"Nothing to do with it?"

"I mean he doesn't know I'm a killer."

"Neither do you, Jim. Snap out of it. If you are going to Niesner for treatment, you ought to tell him about this hallucination."

"No, I wouldn't do that," Boad said in swift alarm. "He wouldn't like that." He stared at Scott. "He wouldn't like me telling you, either." His face paled and a dew of perspiration broke out on his brow. "Promise me you won't tell him, Scott. Promise me that you won't give me away." He reached out a trembling hand and touched Scott's shoulder.

"All right, I won't tell him." Scott gazed at Boad. "Jim, you realize that you are in a bad way. Spend the night here with me. We'll straighten it all out in the morning. We'll work out a rest leave for you. Give you a chance to get hold of yourself."

"Rest leave? Leave Rome? No I couldn't do that," Boad began to get excited again.

"Very well," Scott's tone was soothing. "We won't do anything you don't want to do. Just take it easy here and we'll sort it all out tomorrow.

"Maybe I ought to get on home, Scott."

"Why? Stay here. I'll enjoy the company."

The crafty look stole over Boad's face. "You trying to box me in?"

"Of course not."

"You going to make me stay?"

"No. Do whatever you wish."

Boad gazed about the room uncertainly. "O.K. O.K., that's O.K. O.K., fair enough." He laid down on the bed and closed his eyes. "I'll just relax here a minute, Scott, old chum, then I'll move along. I had to talk with someone, you know. I got a little panicky. Feel better now, though. Under control. Under control." His voice faded away as he dozed off. He was still asleep when Scott flipped off the lights and left to meet Lani.

The first half of the concert was performed under a cloudless sky in the soft silver light of a three-quarter moon. The Forum lay silent and mysterious under the moonlight as the gentle music of Brahms and Mozart floated outward from the ruins of the basilica. After the intermission the mood changed and as the stirring first theme of Beethoven's Fifth Symphony thundered forth, an answering muted roll of thunder was heard in the distance beyond the Palantine Hill, accompanied by lightning flashing intermittently along the horizon. The symphony progressed, and the storm grew closer until flashes of stronger lightning illuminated the edges of thunderheads piling up to the south. As the concert ended, a rush of cool air preceding the rain moved across the Forum. They hurried toward the street exits buffeted by small whirls of dusty air that blew bits of debris against their ankles.

Scott took Lani's arm and motioned toward a rank of horse-drawn carriages. They ran before the rain which was slowly pelting them with big drops and reached the security of the carriage just as torrents of water descended. The driver, already swathed in oilskins, handed them a thick fur rug for their knees and receiving Scott's instructions swung the carriage around in the direction of Via dei Fori Imperiali.

The rain shower was intense, but brief, and the racing storm clouds soon passed overhead leaving a sky of broken clouds and moonlight. The carriage rolled along through the puddles left by the rain, horse and driver both enduring their dampened state stoically. Scott put his arms around Lani and her warm lips found his.

They were finishing a cold soup at Doney's when the waiter handed Lani a small folded piece of paper. She unfolded it, glanced at the message written on it and then somberly tore up the paper, letting it fall into the deep metal ashtray before her.

"What is it?"

"You can't guess?"

"No. Why should I?"

"The man we had on your man, Boad, was found last night in the Borghese Gardens in a garden tool shed. He had been strangled to death." She noticed an expression move behind Scott's eyes and her voice sharpened. "You knew about this, didn't you?"

"No. I had no idea until you spoke."

Her eyes continued to fix his. "I can see that this liaison with you is a mistake." She arose. "I'm leaving."

"I'll take you to the Flora."

"No thank you."

"Lani, you don't think . . ."

"I don't know what to think. Until I have thought this out I don't want to subject myself to your . . . your physical appeal."

He looked hurt and she almost relented, but she took her purse and with a restraining gesture of her hand left him.

Scott sat staring at the tablecloth, a cold feeling of apprehension growing within him. He had to get back to Jim Boad. He threw some bills on the table and left the restaurant. Boad was not in his hotel room, but Scott found a note: "I'm going home. Here's a key in case you need it." There was no signature.

The taxicab dropped him in front of Boad's apartment building within five minutes. He took the creaky elevator to Boad's floor, and walked down the dim hallway to Boad's apartment. He inserted the key in the door and swung it open. He found what he had expected to find. Boad's body was sprawled across the bed with a gaping gunshot wound in the head.

.13.

Scott sat at the end of the garden overlooking Lake Zürich. The book in his hand and the drink nearby on the green metal table suggested that he was a carefree visitor relaxing in the warm spring sunshine among the beds of tulips and daffodils. He looked up and smiled casually as Ernie Sessena dropped into the metal chair beside him. "Good trip?"

"Not bad. I've got a stiff neck from trying to sleep sitting up and my usual sore gut from the food. Otherwise, O.K." He looked down the long stretch of green lawn leading to the Hotel Baur au Lac. "Nice spot. I like Switzerland."

"Yes."

Sessena lit a cigarette. "I don't like what I know, though. Tell me more."

Scott talked earnestly for a few minutes in a low voice. "I suggested this meeting because we have to decide whether or not we zero in on Niesner," he concluded.

Sessena pulled at an earlobe and thoughtfully squinted into the sun. "The startling fact that emerges out of all of this is that both of these guys were patients of old Doc Niesner. That's stretching coincidence too far, says I."

"They not only knew him, but they both showed signs of intense mental strain. Regarding Fenwick, I only have hearsay, though it was confirmed from more than one unrelated source, but with Boad I saw it first-hand. He was rapidly cracking up. He may even have strangled the Israeli agent without remembering it fully."

Sessena pushed out his cigarette and slowly unwrapped a piece of chewing gum, gazing solemnly out on the blue lake with its white sailing boats. He put the gum into his mouth and continued to look into the distance. Finally his eyes swung back to Scott. "I see it this way. We have two agents, one in Bucharest and one in Rome. The agent in Bucharest is a cutie, he dabbles in the refugee traffic, he sets up a double cross for a Syrian revolutionary leader, and he has an affair with a woman spy for Israel. He suddenly leaves Bucharest by train for Switzerland or points West with the Arabs, the Israelis, the mistress and the refugee housemother all tagging along. Under the circumstances he's lucky he only took a header out of the train.

"The agent in Rome, in comparison, is a pretty dull guy. He just thinks he killed someone and in a fit of remorse shoots himself." Sessena chewed thoughtfully on his gum. "Now, this isn't the first time we've lost an agent who played it fast and loose. It isn't the first time we've lost an agent who can't stand himself any longer.

It is the first time we've lost two agents who were under treatment by a psychiatrist . . . and the same psychiatrist at that. And by the way, the Israeli gal is right, they both were filing anti-Israeli intelligence reports. We still can't say if they were phony or not." He glanced at Scott, "I'll fly back to Washington tonight and we'll check what we have on Niesner at McLean. This is over my head at the moment. You may as well fly back to Vienna. I'll be in touch when we've decided on the next step."

Five days later Scott had been ordered back to Italy by an encoded message from Washington and sat on the terrace of the Hotel Splendido at Porto Fino enjoying a luncheon salad after a fast game of tennis on the hotel's red clay court with the Splendido's tennis instructor. As he gazed out over the blue sea with hooded eyes he looked relaxed, even sleepy. In fact, he was impatiently waiting for the hands of the Swiss chronometer on his wrist to point to two o'clock.

A soft breeze ruffled his hair. He yawned hugely, stretched, and reaching for his camera on the table beside his plate, swung it over his shoulder and started down the curving, flower-bordered path to the village.

The scent of salt water and fish touched his nostrils as he walked across the cobbled surface of the market square to the long stone jetty. The hills rising steeply on three sides of the harbor cut off the fresh breeze that was making white caps on the sea outside. The imprisoned air, warmed by the hot sun, hung heavily. The limpid water, appearing amber above the brown stones and mud of the harbor bottom, lapped gently against the stones of the jetty. Somewhere, perhaps on one of the yachts, a radio suddenly blared music and then was choked off in mid-bar.

A teen-aged boy, tanned and bare to the waist above faded denim trousers, stood up in a dinghy which was quietly gliding shoreward on its earlier momentum and leaped effortlessly up to the jetty holding a light mooring line in his hand. Grinning at Scott, he landed on the flat stone surface, his bare feet making a soft smacking sound.

"I have come for you, *signore*." He thrust a hand into the hip pocket of his trousers and handed Scott a soiled card. Written on it was "Sessena."

"Good," Scott said. "I'm ready." He was still wearing his tennis shoes and stepped into the dinghy from the damp stones without difficulty. He sat in the stern feeling the heat of the sun-warmed planking as the boy sat down by the oarlocks and began to row out into the harbor. They progressed among the boats toward the harbor mouth. Around a point of land, invisible from the town but still sheltered from the open sea, was a weathered-looking yawl. Its once white hull was yellowed and its furled sails looked gray and patched. The boy swung the dinghy under its bow and boating his inboard oar brought the boat alongside a small gangway. He sprang onto the gangway and with a few movements of his wrist secured the dinghy's mooring line. "This way, *signore*," he flashed a quick smile at Scott and preceded him onto the deck of the yawl. Scott stepped into the cockpit and down a short ladder to the stateroom. Sessena stood grinning at him.

"Welcome, Scottie, to the smallest and scruffiest unit in the United States Fleet, now under charter to Commodore Sessena." He shook Scott's hand and turned to his companion. "This is Heindrich Brune, Hal to you. I asked him to join us on this one."

Scott nodded at Brune and shook hands.

"Beer all around?" Sessena asked, and on receiving affirmative nods took three cans from a small ice locker. He opened them, each can giving a soft hiss, and passed them around. He dropped into an aluminum chair and faced Brune and Scott as they sat side by side on a leather-cushioned bench which also served as the cover for a gear locker.

Sessena tipped up his can of beer and took several swallows. "Scottie, Hal is a professor of psychology at the University of Chicago, your alma mater. He took a doctor's degree at the University of Vienna in psychology as a young man before emigrating to the States. He is an expert, *the* expert in the States, on intracerebral electrical stimulation. This is a field of scientific research in which the Russians may be away ahead of us. To us laymen it's 'mind bending' or 'thought control.' The idea appeals more to their kind of society than to ours. In any event, they have been in the field for several decades. The idea appealed to the Nazis, too, as you might expect. After the fall of Berlin in 1945 when both sides were grabbing German rocket experts, the Russians also grabbed some experts in the infant theory of mind bending. One of the best, or the worst, in this field, depending upon how you look at it, was Dr. Klaus von Benz." He paused and took another swallow of beer. Dr. Klaus von Benz, we believe, is now Dr. Anton Niesner. Niesner appeared in Vienna two years ago as a refugee from the Communist regime in Romania. He began a modest practice as a psychiatrist. He seems to have been very successful," he added dryly. "He's also opened a clinic in Rome and has a consulting practice throughout Europe."

Brune turned pale gray eyes set in a craggy, sandy face toward Scott. "I was fascinated and alarmed by what Mr. Sessena and his colleagues at CIA told me about your report concerning Boad and Fenwick," he said in faintly British English. "There is every reason to believe that they were the victims of a mind bending effort, not altogether successful in either case, it seems."

Scott nodded, slowly. "I was afraid of something like that."

Brune crossed his long thin legs and placing his beer on a low table nearby, slid down on the bench in what was evidently a characteristic half slouch and began to fill his pipe with stained fingers.

"You see, gentlemen, this is a very old subject. As long ago as 1903, the first year of successful heavier than air flight, by the way, a Russian, Vladimir M.

Bekhterev, wrote a book on reflexology entitled *Foundations of the Theory of the Functions of the Brain*. Research in flight progressed much faster than research in mind bending, but progress has been made, both in the United States and in Russia. We have developed on both sides of the Atlantic a method called ESB or Electrical Stimulation of the Brain. This has its prosaic medical uses, such as in the treatment of epilepsy. We have mounted small metal antennae in the top of the skulls of monkeys, for example, and can control their simple movements by means of a hand transmitter."

Brune's pipe went out and he paused to light it.

"However, ESB takes us only a very short distance toward our goals. To truly control the human mind, electrically that is, to do more than create simple muscular responses such as we have done in monkeys, we must control memory and condition responses."

"Wipe the mind clean, you mean," Scott said.

Brune beamed at him. "Exactly. Exactly. Wipe the mind clean like a slate, so to speak. Of course, we don't need to wipe everything out. That would be counter-productive. We only concern ourselves with the immediate area of memory and response that interests us. Now, again on both sides of the Atlantic, we have developed EDOM or Electronic Dissolution of Memory. You see, gentlemen, the basis of stored memory is a neutral transmitter substance called acetylcholine which exists at a synapse, which separates one nerve cell from another. The EDOM technique builds up through radio waves an excess of acetylcholine at the synapse so that it can't transfer excitation from one cell to another. In other words, it blocks memory and affects the time sense."

"These experiments have been on animals?"

"For the most part. We have had some limited experiments in the United States with human beings, but they have been for narrowly defined medical purposes with the consent of the patient." Brune sighed. "The Russians have had a much broader field of experimentation, you see; using human beings, going well beyond the goals of medical or psychiatric treatment."

Sessena opened another can of beer all around.

"The most exciting development in this field occurred," Brune continued, sipping his beer, "when L. L. Vasiliev, a professor of physiology at the University of Leningrad, developed RHIC, or Radio Hypnotic Intracerebral Control. This is what we call post-hypnotic suggestion triggered at will by radio transmission. In other words, the subject is hypnotized and a certain mental relationship created. This hypnotic state is related to electric or radio impulses. The subject is then brought out from the hypnotic state. Later the hypnotic state is reinduced automatically at intervals by radio control." Brune spread his hands and smiled at them. "In simple, layman's language, that is all we know."

"You think, Professor Brune, that Board was under this sort of hypnosis?"

"Something of that nature. Dr. Niesner, nee von Benz, is one of the world's experts in this field. He has gone far beyond Vasiliev in developing RHIC. How far, we don't know."

"You mean that they can create walking zombies by hypnosis and radio control?"

"Hardly that," Brune laughed deprecatingly. "They obviously had less than complete control over Fenwick and Boad. Both of them seem to have broken away from complete discipline."

Sessena and Scott were silent while Brune carefully refilled his pipe and lit it.

"Were their deaths suicide?" Sessena asked Brune.

"Quite possibly. It has always been the assumption that a person subject to hypnosis cannot be made to do things contrary to his nature. However, hypnosis in that sense is really quite primitive, a relation with the mind of the subject that is basically voluntary; in a sense, self-induced. RHIC is something quite different. Through radio impulses related to past experience through hypnosis we are getting close to the very elements of brain stimuli. They may well pose a problem relating to the brain's past stimulation or capacity to store experience. An irreconcilable conflict, so to speak, which might be resolved by the subject resorting to suicide." Brune smiled at Scott. "Your description of your conversations with Boad suggest that he was the victim of this conflict, and perhaps a victim of dissolution of memory as well. That has to be handled very carefully."

"He was in mental agony. I can see that now. Poor bastard."

"No doubt. I am afraid he was the victim of an incomplete experiment."

"Incomplete?"

"You appeared on the scene before he was ready."

"Ready?"

"Ready to perform at the bidding of Dr. Niesner. At that time there would have been no mental conflicts." Brune puffed on his pipe. "I rather imagine that Fenwick was a similar case. This Israeli woman, the intelligence agent, apparently confronted him in Bucharest much as you did Boad in Rome. By the way," he added, "I would like to sit down with you and reconstruct your conversations with Boad as completely as possible for my records."

Scott nodded. He lit a cigarette and exchanged a brief glance with Sessena. "Not a pretty story, is it, Scottie?" Sessena said.

"Damnable, if you ask me. What were they up to, Ernie?"

Sessena stood up under the low deck and placed his hands in his pockets. "They were trying to create push-button spies," he said softly.

Scott stared. "Push-button spies?"

Sessena nodded. "Let's take it for granted that Niesner has perfected RHIC. He moves West under an elaborate cover as a refugee and practices medicine in Vienna and later in Rome. Why? What stakes are worth the effort and the risk? Only the penetration of our intelligence network on a broad scale. If he can create a few push-button spies, eventually they can break our codes, disrupt our operations, betray our operatives, perhaps assassinate our leaders. He was starting Boad and Fenwick out by ordering them to file false reports on Israel. If we believed it, fine. Otherwise, it at least showed he could control them. The important assignments would come later."

"I don't think he can do that," Scott said slowly.

"Why not?" Sessena asked. "The professor says that it is possible. Not zombies, mind you, or mechanical men, but an otherwise rational, normal person who can be trained through hypnosis to react in a programmed way by means of radio-directed stimulus."

Brune nodded. "Quite feasible. Yes. I am certain that is what Niesner was up to."

"I still say it is impossible," Scott insisted stubbornly. "Man is more than a set of electrical impulses. He has a soul and a will. No, Niesner will never be able to destroy a man's will and his soul and order him about like a robot. Feeding Boad and Fenwick false information on Israel is one thing, making them robots is something else again."

"Why not robots in the limited sense I've described?" Brune asked easily. "I've explained the principle. It's well known."

"There are several thousand years of human civilization that says you are wrong, Professor Brune, and several religions. They say the body dies and the soul or spirit lives on eternally. You contend the opposite. The technique you describe kills the spirit, destroys the soul, and the body lives on. If true, it will disorient mankind. It means that we are only soulless mortal beings in a Godless universe. It strikes me as science's ultimate assault on the human being. I find it repugnant."

Brune waved his pipe and shrugged with a smile. "So be it. Science against faith. It's an old struggle. We won't solve it here today."

Sessena lit a cigarette. "What about Boad and Fenwick, Scottie? How else do you explain their actions?"

"I don't say Niesner wasn't up to something. I just say that he didn't succeed and that he couldn't have succeeded. He was trying to play God, to alter the basic nature of a man."

"Well," Sessena said slowly, "you may be right, but we have to move in on Niesner. That's why Professor Brune is aboard. He's going to work with us."

There was a prolonged silence. Sessena seemed hesitant to continue. At last he cleared his throat and busied himself with lighting a cigarette. "What we want you to do, Scottie, now that you understand the whole problem, is to present yourself to Niesner as a patient and encourage him to use RHIC on you." Sessena's face was without expression when he glanced at Scott after speaking.

Scott wet his lips. "You mean go through this whole mind bending bit? All the way?"

"Yes. You'll take the treatments and then visit Brune to be debriefed, so to speak. We'll learn from you the techniques Niesner has developed. This will be very important scientific information. Brune will help you to cope with the psychological strain of all this. We aren't minimizing it. We know it won't be slight. Brune will help you simulate the correct reactions. When Niesner thinks you're ready, off you go on his orders, but you're ours, not his. That is going to make one hell of a difference."

Scott was silent. "What if I crack up like Fenwick and Boad?"

"We don't think you will. You'll have Brune's help."

Brune pounded the cold ashes from his pipe into the palm of his hand. "You have a strong physique and a well-balanced personality. And you have your faith in man's uniqueness and in his immortality. That will help you. I say that quite sincerely."

"This is asking quite a bit, Ernie."

"I know it. But how else are we going to cope with this situation? We can't let him pick his next subject unknown to us. We have to put a cuckoo in Niesner's nest."

Scott's grin was wry. "No personal reference intended, I suppose?"

The laughs broke the tension.

Scott sat silently for a few minutes, then he exhaled slowly, "O.K. I'll do it. In the line of duty."

"In the line of duty, Scottie. It's the only reason I could ask." Sessena did not smile. He turned to a small pull-down desk behind him and then handed Scott a claim check. That number is a telephone number. Telephone it after your first contact with Niesner. You'll get your instructions. Otherwise, carry on as usual. Your excuse for staying on in Rome is to substitute temporarily for Boad. Washington will send you orders to that effect."

"Niesner will know I'm CIA. I haven't been using a cover."

"That's the idea. You're just what he wants. Incidentally, the Israeli girl is harmless. Let her continue to play at Middle-Eastern cowboys and Indians. Keep close to her. Love her up. If you give the impression you're involved in a love affair, it casts you in a weak light with Niesner. It suggests that you're not seriously at work."

"Sex is also a good antidote for the mental strain you will be under," Brune added. "If you have a woman to accommodate you, take full advantage of it."

"How do I get ashore?" Scott asked shortly.

"The kid will row you back. He's laying off a hundred yards, waiting."

"Where do you go?"

"We go ashore later. You don't think I'd take a chance in this tub in open water, do you?"

.14.

The receptionist's voice over the telephone was vague and disinterested. "The doctor rarely takes new patients except on referral from other doctors. He insists on time for his research and teaching."

"You mean that I can't make an appointment?"

"I am afraid not. The doctor has a clinic on Friday mornings. If you present yourself there, the doctor or one of his assistants might be able to see you, but I can't promise anything. We really recommend another psychiatrist. Then, if there is anything of interest to Dr. Niesner in your case, he could consider it, at the request of your doctor, as a consultant."

"You won't let me speak to Dr. Niesner directly?"

"I am afraid that is impossible, *signore*."

"May I leave a message for the doctor?"

"If you wish."

"I know his patient, James Boad, is dead. Therefore he should be able to take me as a patient."

There was a moment of silence. "What is your name, *signore*?" The tone was even, but no longer disinterested.

"Scott. Robert Scott."

"Your address?"

"Room 208. Hotel Excelsior."

"I shall give your message to the doctor." The connection cut off with a sharp click, leaving only a faint humming sound in the receiver. Scott put the telephone back in its cradle, put on a tie and coat, and took an elevator to the lobby. He stepped out on Via Veneto and began to move with the crowd that flowed down toward Piazza Barberini.

That should do it. They would check him out now. They would learn who he was, if they did not know already. They would decide if they could use him. If they felt they could not, they would probe to decide how much he knew or guessed about Doctor Niesner. Then they would either ignore him or try to kill him. He had to play it just right. With both Fenwick and Boad gone, Niesner would be anxious to ensnare another American intelligence agent for his experiments. But he would be aware of the risks. Niesner would know that American intelligence was investigating the deaths of Boad and Fenwick. He couldn't hope to put Niesner's suspicions completely at rest. The most he could do was to dangle himself before Niesner as another subject for mind bending and to make the risks seem acceptable to him, to use against the doctor his arrogant self-confidence in his method.

Brune had this same intellectual arrogance which minimized belief in any non-scientific possibility outside the scientific theory, particularly if it involved human nature. All scientists, and those whose intellectual disciplines were not scientific, such as economists

.168.

and political "scientists," but who professed to see all truth in scientific or pseudo-scientific disciplines, shared this weakness. He would have to play on this weakness adroitly, to so encourage Niesner's desire for a fitting subject for his experiments that he would reject the "unscientific" possibility that his subject was maintaining an independent will and was, in fact, his nemesis, a counterspy, engaged in a struggle on a new field of battle. It would take finesse. From this struggle, Brune wanted scientific data, Sessena wanted to meet a threat to American espionage, but Scott wanted to resolve a question of fundamental and overriding importance. Can the human soul be captured and enslaved through the human mind and its independent will extinguished, or is each human being unique, and being unique, capable of rejecting the most insidious scientific method in reasserting independence of thought and will?

Scott's thoughts raced on, weighing the philosophical implications of the struggle he had undertaken. Through the centuries, man, aware of his mortality, knowing alone among living creatures that he must die, has sustained his spirit by a religious belief and faith in his uniqueness, a faith that some part of his being resists the limitations of physical existence and lives on, immortal, in another form after death.

The growth of science, the growth of technology, encouraged for the comfort of man, inevitably seeks its ultimate triumph, the destruction of all unscientific

.169.

theory and unscientific possibility, and this must include the destruction of faith in man's uniqueness and immortality, that most unscientific of beliefs, but the one upon which civilization rests.

Niesner and the political systems that support the Niesners would deny to man his one solace as he acknowledges the inevitability of his physical destruction, the inevitability of a lessening zest and enjoyment of life ending in the grave; the belief that his spirit, his soul, cannot be reached or destroyed by earthly powers.

Scott walked through the sun-dappled streets of Rome, sensuously enjoying the sensations of life in the spring in the oldest of Western cities, while a cold, clammy sensation of fear rested in his stomach. He had undertaken to put his belief in his human uniqueness against scientific method, knowing that two men, not unlike himself, had been destroyed in the effort to enslave their wills.

He knew as he walked down the noisy, colorful streets, full of life as only Italian streets can be full of life, that he did not want the appointment with Niesner. He wanted to retreat from this battlefield and fight on more familiar terrain and encounter known terrors. He did not want to fight the lonely battle of psychiatry far, far away from the familiar things that sustain courage and reason and faith. He remembered Jim Boad's tortured eyes, the confused, desperate, lost animal that peered from them and he was afraid. A cold, chill fear settled over him that the sun of the Italian spring could not warm.

He had a sandwich and a glass of iced tea for lunch outside at Doney's. He was about to leave his table when he noticed Lani Evron sitting alone some distance away at a table placed in the sun. She was wearing sunglasses and intently reading a paperback book propped up in front of her as she slowly ate a fresh, crisp-looking salad.

"May I join you?" he asked.

She looked up and smiled. "How nice, Bob. I've missed you for some days now." She put the book into her purse.

"Am I a friend or an enemy?"

"You could be both," her eyes were invisible behind the glasses, "but I've taken you as a lover, nevertheless, and I've missed you," she repeated.

"That could be foolish."

"Yes."

"Have you found out who killed your man?"

"We both know who killed him."

"Yes. I guess we do."

"Why did he do it, Bob?"

"I don't know."

"I hear he shot himself afterward."

"So I understand."

"Remorse?"

"I doubt it."

"Part of my job is over."

"Yes?"

"The American agents sending anti-Israeli false reports have stopped filing the reports."

"I see."

"The other part of my job remains."

"Which is?"

"Convincing the Americans that we did not kill their agents and that the anti-Israeli reports were false." She smiled, "Fortunately you are the one I must convince, I think."

"It won't be easy," he smiled.

"Let me try."

"Please do."

She leaned over and kissed him. "I am so glad to see you, *liebling*. It's been lonely. I am not suited to be a Joan of Arc."

"Why don't we drive to the beach at Ostia and forget that we are spies?"

"I'd love it. Is it warm enough?"

"If it isn't, we'll stay out of the water and make love on the sand."

She smiled and then a little shadow fell across her face. "How long can we play together, darling?"

"I don't know."

She looked at him earnestly, "We enjoy each other while we can?"

He nodded.

"And then?"

He looked at her seriously. "Who knows?"

She arose and took his hand, standing close to him. He was aware of the scent from her hair as she looked up at him. "This is hell, darling. A sweet, pure hell."

"A sweet, pure hell," he agreed.

The beach at Ostia was warm under the hot sun, but the seawater, breaking in a lazy white surf, was cold. They were almost alone on the sand. A few sunbathers were scattered at some distance and here and there a few of the bright multicolor canvas screens of summer had been erected providing a tentative and early splash of gay atmosphere.

Lani sat on their blanket, carefully rubbing a sun lotion on her arms and legs. "Why are you back in Rome, Bob? I thought you had returned to Vienna." She spoke into a silence that had only been accentuated by the sounds of the wind and surf and the occasional harsh cry of a sea gull soaring from the blue water on a sudden updraft of air.

He rolled over on his side from his back and looked at her. "I like it here. I like the company. It was lonely in Vienna. It seems a good time to take a holiday."

She was silent as she rubbed the lotion into the calf of one of her legs. When she had finished she wiped her hands on a towel and regarded him soberly while sitting cross-legged. "You won't confide in me?"

"No."

"You still think we had something to do with Fenwick's death, don't you?"

"No, as a matter of fact, I don't."

"Boad?"

"No, Boad neither. But," he added slowly, "it doesn't always matter what I think."

"I see." She took a small mirror out of her bag and examined her face before carefully applying lipstick. "If your superiors still suspect Israel, aren't you taking a risk being seen with me?"

He grinned. "A guy has to take some risks."

She dropped the lipstick into her bag and laid down beside him, playfully ruffling his hair with one hand. They lay side by side for a moment, gazing deeply into one another's eyes, then he pulled her body against his and their lips met in a long kiss.

She drew her face back a few inches and then rubbed his nose a few times with hers. "You look very winning wearing my lipstick," she murmured.

"It's good for chapped lips."

"Um." Her lips met his softly, gently, without passion, then they slowly firmed and became hard and demanding only to relax again in a suggestion of sexual submission.

"Darling?" She held him tightly and whispered in his ear.

"Yes."

"What are you going to do about Dr. Niesner?"

"I don't know."

"Surely you aren't going to forget him?"

"No, I won't forget him." He released her and rolled to his feet, looking for his cigarettes in the pocket of his folded trousers. He offered her a cigarette and lit it from his own. "So far as we know, he is only a doctor, a practicing psychiatrist."

"Fenwick and Boad were his patients. Both are dead and Boad was a murderer," she reminded him.

"Yes. He seems to be a lousy doctor."

She looked at him with annoyance. "Don't treat me like a woman."

"I wouldn't dream of it," his grin broadened.

She laughed in spite of herself. "Intellectually, I mean." Her face became intense again. "You know both of these men were being used by somebody."

"Why Niesner? He's an improbable spy master."

"I am certain that he is an agent of the Arabs," she said firmly.

"Perhaps." His tone was indifferent.

"You are exasperating," she said, emphasizing the word and drawing it out. Her eyes narrowed. "Perhaps on purpose."

"Don't be a nag," he said lightly. He moved toward the water. "I'm going to take a dip," he said over his shoulder, leaving her gazing after him with an unfathomable expression in her eyes.

.15.

The next day he received the telephone call. "Dr. Niesner can see you," the receptionist's brisk, impersonal voice said, "If you can come this afternoon at five o'clock. It will be a short, exploratory interview only. Then the doctor can advise you and perhaps refer you to another doctor."

"That's wonderful!" Scott said with false enthusiasm. "Thank you very much. I'll be there at five."

The receptionist gave him the familiar address, with an admonition to be prompt, and hung up.

Scott stared at the telephone, his pulse racing. This was it. If he handled it right, he was in. His damp palms told him that he wished he had failed to get the appointment.

He entered the slim shaft of cement and glass through the tiny lobby between the stores and took a self-service elevator to the tenth floor. It was five minutes to five.

The elevator opened onto a reception room corresponding in size to the main floor lobby. Niesner evidently had the entire floor. The receptionist was a cold-eyed, composed woman of about thirty with classical Roman features. She glanced up as the elevator door opened.

"Mr. Scott?"

Scott nodded. "Yes. Robert Scott."

"Please sit down. The doctor will see you in a few minutes."

Scott sat down on a modern-style settee of dull black leather supported by chromium legs. He noticed that there were no magazines or newspapers in the reception room and no pictures on the plain white walls. There were two chairs similar in design to the settee. The receptionist's desk, of a thick pressed wood covered with walnut veneer on a chromium frame, furnished the only color contrast in the room. Even the receptionist had black hair and eyes and was dressed in a black silk suit with a white blouse.

Promptly at five o'clock a door opened from an interior room and an athletic-looking male orderly dressed in a white medical smock entered and wordlessly took a slip from the receptionist. He turned to Scott unsmilingly. "Mr. Scott? This way please." He spoke with a faint, unidentifiable accent.

Scott followed him through the door. They turned and walked down a hall to the rear of the building. A heavy door with a massive tumbler lock opened into a warm, sunlit room. Its far wall was of glass. Through the glass, from which transparent curtains and draperies had been drawn back, Scott looked out over Rome bathed in a golden sunset. The attendant withdrew and Scott was left alone. There was no suggestion in the room of a doctor's office. It was tastefully and warmly furnished in a modern Scandinavian style with none of the starkness found in the reception room.

Scott immediately noticed that the room was absolutely quiet. None of the background sounds of the building with its other tenants or of the noisy city outside were audible. He could hear the faint whir of the motor of an electric clock on a nearby table very clearly.

He walked over to the window and looked out over the city for a moment. Without its sounds and smells, Rome was unnatural, a muted neuter, a scenic backdrop. He did not like the sensation of standing suspended a hundred feet in the air behind thick soundproof glass and turning about, faced into the room and calmly waited for the doctor's arrival, his hands clasped behind his back.

It was nearly five minutes before an energetic, vital man of slightly over middle height walked into the room from the door Scott had entered. His silver-gray hair was brushed straight back from his temples accentuating a high forehead above deep-set dark eyes. He smiled at Scott, and touching a small bristly gray moustache with a forefinger, motioned him to an armchair facing the window.

"I have not really been keeping you waiting, Mr. Scott." He spoke English the way cultivated Viennese speak it. "I have been observing you through the mirror there." He gestured toward a large mirror set in a plain brass frame. "It is a window from the other side."

Scott glanced at the mirror. "Imagine that. I've seen them in the movies, but not in real life."

"I was not being an eavesdropper, you know. It is a technique that enables me to watch a patient without his being aware of it. Clinically speaking, this is most important."

Scott remained silent and the doctor sat down in a chair slightly closer to the window than Scott's own. It had the effect in the strong yellow light of the sunset of throwing the doctor's features into half shadow. Only the crown of silver hair and the steel rims of his glasses remained distinct.

"You seem a healthy enough specimen. Quite poised. No mannerisms. What brings you to me?"

"I suppose it surprises you to have an American intelligence agent ask for psychiatric help?"

Niesner put the tips of his fingers together and answered evenly. "As a doctor, Mr. Scott, nothing surprises me. I am, of course, rather gratified at your frankness. I didn't know intelligence agents identified their profession. It saves a great deal of verbal fencing and time. Time, you know, is valuable, not only because it is limited, but because we don't know how limited it is."

"I'll save us some more time, Doctor Niesner. As I told your receptionist, I know Boad, our CIA agent in Rome, was a patient of yours. I am told that Fenwick, our CIA agent in Bucharest, was also a patient of yours. We both know that they are dead."

There was a short silence. "You are a most surprising person, Mr. Scott," Niesner said at last. "I am very glad that I agreed to see you." He reached for a cigarette box on a low table beside his chair and offered one of the oval-shaped cigarettes to Scott. He accepted Scott's light and sat back in his chair. "How do you imagine that I came to treat two of your colleagues, Mr. Scott?" he asked, removing a grain of tobacco from his tongue with the middle finger of his left hand.

"I have no idea."

"You are not curious?"

"Mildly. But I have my own problems."

"I see. And why do you come to me?"

"Boad spoke highly of you."

"But Boad committed suicide."

"I know, poor guy. He visited me shortly before he died."

"Did he now?"

"Yes. I could see that he was very nervous, but I never imagined that he would kill himself."

"Sometimes these matters resolve themselves that way. We try to channel anxieties in another direction, to suggest other solutions, but if the suicidal complex is too far developed before medical assistance is sought, there is not much we can do. You know that Mr. Boad tried to kill himself twice before he came to me?"

"No. I didn't know that." Scott's voice was indifferent.

Niesner smoked his cigarette for a moment. "Why did you assume Ralph Fenwick was a patient and that I knew that he was dead?"

"An intelligence source told me that Fenwick was a patient of yours and saw you frequently in Vienna and in Rome."

"And why would I know that he is dead?"

"The source said that you were a Russian agent and may have been responsible for his death," Scott smiled deprecatingly.

"How extraordinary!" Niesner said. "And what do you think, Mr. Scott?"

"I certainly don't believe that kind of nonsense. Otherwise, I wouldn't be here as a patient."

Niesner studied him silently for several minutes. "As a matter of fact, I did know about poor Fenwick's death," he spoke somberly, "but he was not a patient. Ralph Fenwick was one of the best friends, one of the greatest benefactors I ever had. I owe my life to him. He ransomed me from behind the Iron Curtain and brought me out to Vienna two years ago. I am one of dozens he rescued from Romanian prison farms. I was fortunate. When I fell from favor because of my German ethnic background and my political views, I was at least allowed to practice my profession among the other prisoners, as a medical doctor, not as a psychiatrist," he smiled. "I did not have to undermine my health in manual labor like the others. I even had raw material for my psychiatric studies from among my fellow unfortunates. In time, through an angel of mercy named Magda Stanescu, Ralph Fenwick arranged to ransom me for fifteen thousand dollars and brought me to Vienna. Of course, I saw him often wherever I could thereafter. He was one of my dearest friends. When he fell from that train, my refugee friends let me know at once." He looked earnestly at Scott. "I tell you, Mr. Scott, there are scores like me that mourn Ralph Fenwick in silence. We can't speak of this great soul to the world because we would compromise the network of Magda Stanescu which brings refugees to the West each week."

Scott wondered if he knew that both Magda Stanescu and Franz were dead.

Niesner arose from his chair and poured two glasses of sherry at a sideboard. He placed one, unbidden, by Scott's chair and resumed his seat. "Of course, I knew Fenwick was in your CIA as well. For this reason, I tried to help poor Boad when he came to me and this is why I agreed to see you. I think I owe some of my skills to the colleagues of Ralph Fenwick if they ask my help."

Scott nodded. "You didn't have to explain this to me, Doctor. The most unreliable information in the world comes from intelligence sources. Informers sometimes can't resist creating the information they sell. I'm glad you did explain, however. I knew nothing of

Ralph's work with refugees until after his death. Technically, he violated regulations in engaging in this work, but it was humanitarian and I am proud to learn of it."

Niesner sipped his sherry. "I am afraid we have gotten away from the doctor-patient relationship in talking of a mutual friend. What is it that brings you to me, Mr. Scott, in a professional capacity?"

Scott cleared his throat. "I don't quite know how to explain it, Doctor. I have a growing sense of depression, a sense of guilt. I am a civilized man, a graduate of a liberal arts college and a law school, a linear descendant of the Western traditions of culture. Yet, I am engaged in espionage. I steal, I lie, I betray, I kill as a part of my job. I am, in fact, licensed by my government to revert to the laws of the jungle. To subvert, if necessary in a particular case, everything Western civilization and my country stands for. I watch my country at home and abroad lose its way. I've lost my way. What is it all about? Everyday I get more and more depressed. I'm afraid I'll crack up, just like Boad did. We talked about this a couple of times before he died, sort of comparing notes on how we felt, and when he killed himself, well, Doctor, it was kind of like being left alone with the problem, you know? And then I got scared. Damn scared. I can't quit espionage, you know, anymore than Boad could have. They don't let us do that. Once you're in, you're in, if you know what I mean. Then I thought of you. Jim spoke so highly of you, like a father almost, and I thought I'd come to you; that maybe you could set me straight—give me help."

Niesner's voice was gentle. "I'm not a substitute for a father, Mr. Scott, or for a priest either. I don't offer a religion or a philosophy. I am a medical doctor. There are limits to what I can do. I can't remake the world for you. I can't give you absolution for your sins."

"Yes. I know that." Scott's voice was subdued as he rubbed his hands together. Then, as if recollecting himself, he put a hand on each knee and looked before him stoically.

Niesner studied him at length without speaking further. Then he said softly. "Have you anything else you would like to say?"

"No. I guess that's about it."

"Very well, Mr. Scott. I'm glad you came to see me. You were a friend of Ralph Fenwick so you are a friend of mine. Come to see me the day after tomorrow. We will chat as friends. I will decide later if you need psychiatric help and if I am the doctor for you. There is no need to hurry. We take our time." His voice was warm and reassuring.

"I may have to go back to Vienna in a week or so."

"No problem. I am in Vienna frequently, a doctor of two cities. You are not alone with your thoughts, my friend. Remember that. That is the main thing to remember. You are not alone. You have a friend. You are safe."

Scott sighed. "I feel better already."

"Of course you do. These problems are never as big as they seem." He walked down the hall with Scott to the reception room. The receptionist had gone for the night. "The day after tomorrow at five o'clock." Niesner smiled and nodded a good-by as Scott stepped into the elevator.

.16.

Scott entered a glass-enclosed telephone booth and dialed the number on the claim check.

"Si?"

"Scott."

"Take a taxi to Restaurante Romano. Walk through the kitchen to the back entrance. No one will stop you. Just tell the headwaiter your name. We'll pick you up in the alley." The voice had a faint Italian accent.

"Right."

"It's now six-thirty. Make it seven. If you are followed, shake them and try again on the hour. If you can't make it by ten o'clock, forget it. We'll contact you."

"O.K."

There was a click at the other end of the line.

He stood outside the telephone booth and lit a cigarette. Then he sauntered down the street window-shopping. When he was certain that he was not being followed, he hailed a taxi and got out a block away from Restaurante Romano.

It was early, and except for a couple drinking at the bar, the dimly-lit restaurant was deserted. Scott murmured his name to the headwaiter who casually indicated the swinging doors into the kitchen and continued to study a reservation list. After the noise, light, and heat of the kitchen, the alley was a jet-black well of silence. He stood against the wall of the restaurant, his senses straining. His eyes were just beginning to make out dim shapes in the dark when a hand gripped his upper arm. He was drawn soundlessly toward a battered black sedan. He got into the back seat and the door closed behind him. His guide had disappeared in the darkness. The driver, a silhouette against faint light at the end of the alley, started the car and with the lights off, coasted rapidly down a cobbled incline toward a commercial street. They turned into the street with a roar as the parking lights winked on and the motor accelerated powerfully.

The car took a tortuous route through a confusing maze of streets and braked to a stop before a series of shuttered store fronts. Above the fronts rose ornate five-story apartment facades, semi-elliptical bulwarks extending as far as the eye could see in the dim street lights.

A figure stepped out from the shadow of a building. "Come this way." They entered the dank, close atmosphere of a narrow stairway leading to an upper floor as the sedan pulled away from the curb with a clashing of gears, leaving a blue-gray cloud of exhaust fumes hanging wraith-like in the air.

Scott followed the figure up the creaking stairs to a

landing. A door was unlocked and pushed open before him. "Go right in."

Sessena and Brune were sitting on straight chairs waiting for him. Apart from a similar third chair the room was empty. The four whitewashed walls were bathed in a stark light from a single powerful overhead light bulb.

Scott smiled as the door shut behind him, leaving him alone with Sessena and Brune. "Nice spot you have here. Are we having another economy drive back at McLean?"

"This will be the drill from now on, Scottie," Sessena said. "Each time you leave us we will give you a phony claim check or similar item with a number. That number will be your telephone contact for the next meeting. When you call it you will get your instructions as you did tonight. However, in the future you will be accompanied on your ride and will be blindfolded. We will meet in a different place each time. Sometimes I'll be absent. I have to move about a bit on other assignments, but Brune will be here and it will always be a room just like this one, without distinguishing marks and with the same three chairs. Our team here in Italy will set it up each time, but only we three will know the reason for the meetings."

Scott glanced about him. "I don't get it."

"You are going to be under considerable mental strain from now on," Brune said in matter-of-fact tones. "It is better that your meetings with me or with

.189.

both of us are one uniform experience, as identical as a series of meetings can be, so that they become indistinguishable from each other and tend to blend in your memory into a single whole."

"Why?"

"We will be debriefing you after your meetings with Niesner. We don't want it to work the other way around."

"You think I'll tell him what happens here?"

"Not consciously. No, not at all."

There was a pregnant silence.

"It seems a reasonable precaution, Scottie," Sessena said softly. "We all understand security precautions."

Scott lit a cigarette and after inhaling, studied the glowing end for a moment. "What if I mention your names?"

"They won't mean anything to Niesner. Besides, he won't try to query you on intelligence matters. That would destroy your 'confidence' in him, arouse your suspicions and make you a more difficult subject. His interest will be in providing you with new stimuli," Brune added. "Your only problem will be to guard against the verbal slip, the unexpected or unexplained comment. By making all of our meetings exactly alike this is easier for you to avoid. In time you will come to believe that you have only one meeting to regard as a secret. That is an easier secret to keep than the secret of many meetings."

"O.K." Scott said sourly. "I get the point." He

looked at Sessena. "I'm not used to being treated as a security risk, that's all."

"It's a new ball game, Scottie," Sessena said quietly. "The rules are somewhat different. Don't take it personally. Frankly, this is the most impersonal exercise I've ever gotten into. That's the hell of it." He gazed somberly at Scott.

"Let's turn now to the matter at hand," Brune interjected crisply. "You have just had your first meeting with Doctor Niesner. What happened?"

"We chatted, both busily trying to fool the other. I tried to sell Niesner on the fact that I was a guilt-ridden American agent who was under a mental strain and needed psychiatric help."

"Did he buy it?"

"I don't know," Scott said simply. "I see him at five o'clock the day after tomorrow."

"Good! Good!" Brune slapped one knee. "It's a beginning."

"What was his line to you?" Sessena asked.

"He claims Ralph Fenwick rescued him from behind the Iron Curtain and was a dear friend, not a patient. He took Jim Boad as a patient and may take me as a patient because he feels indebted to Fenwick and feels inclined to help his colleagues."

"Very touching," Sessena said dourly.

Brune filled his pipe from a worn leather tobacco pouch. "You both cleared the air a bit, created the basis for a working relationship. That's very important." He laboriously lit the pipe. "You appear before him as what you are, a CIA agent. You do not regard him with suspicion. On the contrary, you think of him as a source of strength and of help in your emotional, guilt-ridden state. From his point of view it is not unnatural that you should seek out a doctor known to you to be treating a friend. In Communist dialectic all CIA men must be guilt-ridden, so it doesn't surprise him to learn that you are. The problem is Fenwick. If you accept Niesner's story of his devotion and gratitude to Fenwick, then you can accept his alleged motivation for treating Boad and you. Otherwise, he has been involved with two American intelligence agents, both dead and he cannot believe that you, a third agent, will not be suspicious. How did you handle that?"

"I acted sympathetic, but indifferent, as if I were completely concerned with my own problems."

"Splendid." Brune rubbed his hands together. "He wants you, you see? You offer him an unforeseen third chance to create a push-button spy. If he can persuade himself that there is any reasonable basis for your confidence in him as a doctor and in his belief that you are a patient rather than a suspicious agent, he will do so. He will do so within the next forty-eight hours after which you are due to meet again. Otherwise, he will cancel your appointment."

"His suspicions will always remain just beneath the surface, however," Sessena warned. "This setup be-

.192.

tween Niesner and Scott is as touchy as hell," he glanced at Brune.

"Exactly," Brune agreed. "We are nurturing a very fragile relationship." He beamed. "But I think you are handling it very well, Scott. Continue to act as if you are wholly preoccupied with yourself. That's the right approach. You might introduce a few mild neurotic observations or introspections at your next meeting."

Scott nodded.

Sessena handed him a new claim check with a grin. "Those are for the shoes you left. They were in lousy shape."

"How do I leave here?" Scott asked, slipping the claim check into his billfold.

"Just walk down the steps. A car will take you to a bus line, not necessarily the nearest one. There's nothing more disarming than seeing an intelligence agent get off a bus." Sessena squeezed him on the upper arm. "Take it easy, boy."

The staircase seemed darker going down than going up. He waited fifteen minutes at the bus stop until a worn-looking diesel bus appeared, trailing a blue cloud of exhaust fumes. He sat on the shabby vinyl cushion of one of the seats wondering what he would do with himself for the next two days. He had to keep occupied. It would be a mistake to think too much about Niesner. The fear and apprehension he felt had to be ignored, smothered by other more immediate emotions, otherwise Niesner would sense that he regarded him as an adversary, rather than as a doctor.

He got off the bus and soon was surrounded by the bustle of Via Veneto. It was a mild, clear night and the street was thronged with laughing, chattering groups of people. He entered the Excelsior and after buying a package of cigarettes went up to his room. He shaved, took a long hot shower, and dressed in clean clothes. He emerged again on Via Veneto refreshed and relaxed. With relaxation came hunger and the realization that he had not eaten since midday. He walked up the street to Doney's.

His cold cuts and beer had been served when Lani Evron sat down beside him. To his surprise, in addition to pleasure, an emotion of great relief swept over him. She was there smiling at him wordlessly across the table with the easy familiarity she had recently adopted. He then realized that he was falling in love with her and that for the first time that day he felt completely happy and carefree.

"Have you had your dinner?" he asked, a slow grin stealing across his features.

She nodded, still smiling at him. "You are truly glad to see me, aren't you?"

"Yes."

"I can tell by the way your face lit up when you glanced up and saw me."

"I would rather see you than anyone."

"I feel that way too," she said simply. "I called your

hotel room several times, but there was no answer. I hoped that I would find you here."

"You could have left your name. I would have telephoned."

"I was afraid that you wouldn't. Then I would have had no excuse to telephone again. It would have been a matter of pride."

"I would have telephoned. You know that."

"I know it now," she looked at him tenderly. "There is an expression in your eyes that wasn't there before."

"I just realized when I saw you now what you mean to me."

"I feel it too," she murmured.

He paid the check and they walked slowly down the street hand in hand among the other strollers, stopping from time to time before shop windows or theatre marquees, saying whatever came into their heads, laughing at nothing, buoyed toward ecstasy by mere nearness, the touch of hands and bodies, her perfume, his odor of masculine cleanliness, their sudden realization of a mutually shared love.

After nearly an hour of directionless wandering, they entered a small piazza which they had never seen before. At the far end, a fountain ran behind a low, rounded stone wall, a smooth elongated sheet of water lighted by dim lights, falling over a precipice of smooth fitted stone blocks. It ran effortlessly, satin-smooth, the color of onyx traced with green, highlighted with wisps of silver where a rough stone edge or the stirring of the breeze caused a tendril of water to detach itself from the massive stream to catch its own light before it fell with the rest into a huge basin peopled with wet stone dolphins, mermaids, and a family of gargoyles.

They sat on the stone wall, feeling its cool surface beneath their extended palms, listening to the steady flow of the fountain behind them. Lani turned slightly and looked down into the basin. "I like dolphins. They always seem carefree and gay."

"So do mermaids."

"But mermaids are lazy and vain, don't you think? Always sitting on rocks, combing their hair, admiring themselves."

"That is a posture to catch unwary men. They are probably very busy the rest of the time."

"Doing what?" She challenged him.

He laughed. "Whatever mermaids do."

"What about the gargoyles?"

"They look harmless. Rather homely though."

She tilted her head to one side. "Why do you suppose sculptors in the middle ages were so fond of gargoyles?"

"I suppose it expressed their fear of the unknown."

She let him light her cigarette. "We make no gargoyles today, staring up from fountains, peering from church towers, glowering from public buildings. Is it that we have no fears to express?"

"I think our fears are best expressed by nothingness, plain sheets of cold steel, hard, smooth glass colored to prevent the passage of sunlight, air filter systems and sealed windows to lock out the out-of-doors, smooth, gray cement on which nothing is written or drawn or molded. When we wish to express tortured feelings we twist and warp our metals into meaningless shapes and let them rust away on pedestals." He gazed somberly at the stone figures in the fountain. "This is the age of disbelief, of the scoffer, of the nihilist, and our fear is not now of heaven nor of hell, nor of the tortured figures of medieval imagination and superstition. It is a fear of nothingness, meaninglessness. Is this, after all, a world without meaning, peopled by soulless living things that reproduce and die without reason, floating through a dead and silent universe? If it is, the cold slab of tortured, rusting metal worked by today's sculptors serves as well as the stone gargoyles of the middle ages."

She looked into the fountain and shivered. "I prefer the gargoyles. They at least represent life."

"So do I. The known peril is easier to face than the unknown peril." He flexed his fingers together and looked down at the white, straining knuckles. "The most terrible thing to discover, I think," he said slowly, "is that man has no soul and that all of his experience is without meaning. Perhaps our modern art is suggesting that this is true."

She reached out for him. "Let's go home, *liebling*."

They returned to his hotel room. The maid had turned the bed down and a single lamp glowed on a bedside table. Lani extinguished it and moved into his arms. They stood in the faint light coming through the woven glass curtains from the street outside. Her lips found his, warmly and passionately as his arms enfolded her and drew her to him, then they brushed across his cheek to his ear. "I do love you," she whispered. "I do love you."

He opened her blouse and kissed her where the cleavage of her breasts rose above the lace of her lingerie. She pressed his head against her breast and kissed him on his upturned cheek. "It would be better in bed, darling," she whispered after a moment.

They lay together between the cool sheets, her body against his, her head resting on his breast. He could feel a trickle of perspiration from her forehead. His hand gently stroked back her thick hair, feeling its faint dampness, stirring its clean scent.

They had fallen asleep. He was awakened by the flutter of her eyelashes against his cheek.

"Are you awake?" she asked.

"Yes."

"It is different when you are in love," she said after a moment.

"Yes."

"Before it was passion. Now there is a tenderness, a consideration."

"'That's what love is."

"You feel that?"

"Yes."

"It is different," she repeated happily and fell asleep again.

He listened to her regular breathing and watched the play of the shadows in the room as a faint breeze stirred the curtains. It must be near dawn, he thought, and dozed off.

When he awoke he was alone in bed. He turned on his side. She was sitting on a bench before a dressing table slowly brushing her long hair. He watched the rhythmic movement of the brush and the slow sweep of her hair against the soft cream of her back. She sat erect, her head thrown back, her back straight, curving gently into the firm buttocks which rested on the damask cushion. She was beautiful. He gave an involuntary sigh and she turned about with a dazzling smile. "Good morning, darling."

He did not speak but walked over and bending, embraced her, his palms cupping her firm breasts. He kissed her behind the left ear and she straightened with a faint tremble as her left hand rose to stroke the side of his head. "I love you," he said.

"And I love you." She turned and met his lips.

"Breakfast here?"

"Yes. I'm not interested in the world at the moment."

"Croissants, café au lait, orange juice?"

"Please."

He stepped to the telephone and ordered breakfast.

As he stepped into the shower he felt he had never been happier.

They breakfasted by the window. The morning sun flooded the white damask cloth, the cheerful rose motif of the breakfast service, and the warm brown rolls. A small bouquet of three jonquils in a crystal bud vase blended with the pale yellow of butter flakes on ice and the deep orange of the fruit juice. She poured his coffee and milk expertly, the coffee pot in one hand and the milk jug in the other. "Must you do anything today?"

"No."

"We have the day together?"

"Yes."

"All of it?"

"All of it." He smiled.

She stretched ecstatically, pushing her arms before her. "How wonderful." She gazed across the table at him happily, then a faint expression of sadness moved across her eyes. "We'll have each day as it comes, darling? As long as we can?"

He captured one of her hands and kissed it. "Yes."

"It can't be for always?" her voice was half question, half resigned statement.

"I don't see how it can," he said gently.

"Neither do I," she spoke after a moment. "I should not have asked." She was quiet for a while and then forced a gay smile. "We can only live today and we are together today. We will live tomorrow, tomorrow."

He walked around the table to her and brushed

back her hair with one hand before kissing her. "It's an uncertain world, darling, for people like you and me, but we'll make the best of it." He grinned. "After all, if we weren't spies, we never would have met."

Her warm laugh bubbled forth and she briefly put the fingers of one hand to her lips as she looked up into his eyes. "Yes, how lucky we are." She said it without irony.

.17.

Doctor Niesner kept Scott waiting only a few minutes in the consulting room. He entered briskly and nodded pleasantly at Scott, indicating to him the same chair in which he had sat before.

"I thought you would want me to lie down on a couch this time," Scott said with a tentative smile.

"That is the role of the analyst, Mr. Scott. I am a consulting psychiatrist. The techniques are somewhat different." He looked at Scott intently. "How have you spent your time since you were last here?"

"Mostly with a girl friend."

"A Roman girl?"

"No, Israeli." Scott laughed deprecatingly. "I am afraid that she is an agent too."

"I see." The tone of voice was noncommittal. "Do you only feel comfortable among agents?"

"No. I just meet them in my line of work."

"This girl is assigned to Rome by Israel?"

"She is assigned to Bucharest. She was a friend of Ralph Fenwick. She was on the same train when he died."

The eyes looked at Scott intently, unwaveringly. "So your interest in her is not entirely personal?"

"Not exactly."

"What is her interest in you?"

"She believes the United States suspects Israel of killing Fenwick. She wants to know what I know."

Niesner offered Scott one of the oval cigarettes from the box on the table and took one himself. He smoked quietly for a few minutes.

"Do you think I should stop seeing her?" Scott asked in an anxious tone.

"No. Of course not. There is no reason why I should interfere with either your profession or your love life, even," Niesner's eyes twinkled, "if both are a bit unusual."

"I thought I should be perfectly frank with you as my doctor," Scott said defensively.

"Of course. Quite right. It enables us to establish a proper relationship. Tell me, do you suspect this woman of a personal involvement in Fenwick's death?"

"It's possible."

"Are you attracted to her sexually?"

"Yes."

"You are having an affair?"

"Yes."

"You see that creates a certain area of emotional conflict, don't you?"

"Yes I do."

"The conflict between sexual desire and duty?"

"Yes."

"You expressed to me at our first meeting a revulsion against your duties as an intelligence agent."

"Yes."

"You do not feel this revulsion toward this woman?"

"No."

"Why do you suppose that is?"

"She is a very lovely woman."

Niesner extinguished his cigarette and gazed very searchingly into Scott's face, then he shifted his eyes and looked introspectively into the distance.

"Tell me, Mr. Scott, if you could choose another profession, do anything you wished in life, what would you choose to do?"

Scott thought for a moment. "I think I would like to be a teacher," he said slowly. "Or work among the poor as a public defender. I am a lawyer," he added.

"You yearn to perform some public service?"

"At the people-to-people level. What I'm doing now is public service, or so they told me when I was recruited in law school." A note of bitterness crept into his voice.

"Why do you have this desire to serve people?"

"I am lonely, terribly lonely. As a spy I'm set apart from other people. Even in a crowd I am alone because they accept me for one thing when I know I am something quite different. I want to be near to people, to belong to them, to feel a common identity, to be used by them."

Niesner smiled kindly. "You are quite articulate."

Scott's eyes fell shyly to the floor. "I find it easy to talk with you, Doctor. I guess that is why you are in this business."

The electric clock's motor purred audibly in the stillness.

"I think your problem is a simple one, Mr. Scott," Niesner's voice was warm and sympathetic. "You have some entirely understandable emotional conflicts. Fortunately, we are meeting them at an early stage. I think we can work them out together. I want you to have no fears on that account. Mr. Boad's problem was much different than yours, much more complicated."

"That's a relief," Scott sighed.

"A short period of treatment and I am certain you will adjust yourself." Niesner smiled. "You have some decisions to make, Mr. Scott. If I could engage in an unprofessional description, almost an indiscretion," the smile became self-deprecating, "you need help in making up your mind to a course of action. It is indecision, not a mental or nervous problem, that is the source of your unhappiness."

"You make it sound so simple," Scott said.

"It is simple to state, not so simple to resolve; but, not too difficult either with some trained assistance."

"I'll do whatever you say, Doctor."

"Good," Niesner moved his chair closer to Scott's and grasped both his hands in a firm, dry grip. The electric clock buzzed softly, its gold hands at a quarter to the hour. "I want you to look directly into my eyes,

.206.

Mr. Scott, and concentrate entirely on what I am saying to you."

Scott grinned. "This isn't hypnotism, is it, Doctor?"

"It is therapeutic treatment, Mr. Scott." Niesner's voice had an edge of annoyance in it.

"I'm sorry," Scott said contritely.

"Now look into my eyes, Mr. Scott. I want you to think with me for a moment." The intent gray eyes behind the steel-rimmed spectacles came within a few inches of his own. The iris, the pupils, the eyelids dominated all but a peripheral vision that remained aware of the trimmed, bristly gray eyebrows and a mole on the skin under one eye. "The most important thing in the world is to relax, to let tension flow away. Tension is the enemy of man, relaxation is his friend. Ease is our object, complete ease." The dry fingers released their grip on his hands and two index fingers massaged Scott's temples, gently, but with an insistent, firm pressure. "Ease is a lovely word, gentle, melodious, quiet; ease—to say it is like the movement of soft summer air, whispering, whispering, whispering."

"Scott!"

Scott jerked from the reverie into which he was drifting and looked into the smiling eyes of Doctor Niesner. "I'm sorry," he said. "I guess I wasn't paying attention."

"Quite all right," Niesner said cheerfully. "I think that is all for today. Let me see you tomorrow at the same time."

Scott ran a hand through his hair. "We aren't going on?" His voice was disappointed.

"Not today."

Scott adjusted his tie reluctantly. "Fine. Tomorrow, then, at five."

His eyes unconsciously sought the face of the electric clock. With a feeling of cold shock he saw that its hands now pointed to ten minutes past six.

Within the hour he was in another plain, white-washed room with Brune and Sessena. He recounted his conversation with Niesner including the disturbing sense of lost time at the end. "I guess he had me under without my realizing it," he shook his head in self-disgust.

Brune nodded with satisfaction. "The tug of war has begun. Congratulations, Scott. You convinced him that he could take a chance on you as a subject. The right approach is to conceal nothing from him except the most important thing of all, these debriefing sessions."

"Russian intelligence will check you out, believe me, so play it straight," Sessena added. "Play it out just like you are. Suspicion that the Israeli's engineered Fenwick's death, attraction to the Evron woman, bitterness toward your profession, desire for reassurance from Niesner. It makes you the weak, mixed-up guy he is looking for. Now to break you loose for these sessions with our resident head shrinker, we are going to resort from here on in to a stand-in or a decoy to keep your surveillance happy until you get back. If they keep losing you after each session you have with Niesner they will get suspicious."

"What if he asks things in a sensitive area?" Scott fretted.

"He won't," Brune assured him. "As I informed you before, that would be too crude at this stage."

"At this stage?"

"Later, you're supposed to do what he wants," Brune said simply. "However, even then, he will have to handle you very carefully. Your basic loyalties will be very strong."

"Thanks," Scott said dryly.

"I think he will try to orient you toward future events. To try to obtain past intelligence would be to risk a personality conflict which could ruin the experiment. Niesner won't do that. He's much too professional."

"A conflict like Boad's?" Scott asked.

"We don't really know, do we?" Brune replied.

Lani looked at him across the table of the restaurant whose dining room had been moved to the roof as the Roman weather warmed. Under a striped canopy and with the help of candles and flowers, a special magic was created that would last through the summer and into the autumn. "You look tired."

"I am, a little."

"Would you rather I didn't come to you tonight?"

"No. This is no night to be alone."

Her smile was enigmatic as she sipped the red wine in her glass. She held it against the candle flickering inside a small hurricane lamp. "It is a beautiful color. A strong color. The flame of the candle seems to dance in it. It is almost alive."

He held his glass to the candle flame. "Red is a strong color. It is the color of life, violence, and death."

She glanced at him quizzically. "You think of it that way?"

"Sometimes."

"What did you do today, after you left me?"

"I went to the Embassy to check up on a few things."

"I thought you were on holiday?"

"I still have to check up on a few things, especially since Boad died."

"Did you think of me?"

"Of course."

"I thought of you, constantly," her eyes glowed and one hand sought his.

"I'll take you home."

"To my hotel?"

He nodded.

"I like your room better."

"Why?"

"I don't know. It's yours. It's masculine. I feel safer there."

"Perhaps you feel less committed; visiting out, so to speak."

It was as if he had struck her. "That was unkind," she said in an almost inaudible voice.

"I am sorry. That was clumsily put." His effort to smile at her was not successful.

She looked at him with troubled eyes. "What is the matter?"

"Nothing. Nothing at all. I am a little on edge, I guess."

"I don't take you lightly, Bob. It's not like that."

"I know."

"You said last night that you loved me. Why don't you love me truly?" She held up a restraining hand at his glance. "I don't mean love-making, I mean love, trust, sharing, kindness."

He looked at her sadly. "You know we can't have that kind of relationship." Then he added bitterly, "We are spies."

"We are human beings."

"No, we aren't. We feel, move, look like human beings, but something inside is dead, missing, or mislaid."

She deliberately lit a cigarette, controlling with effort a tremor in her fingers. "You make our relationship seem like nothing more than physical hunger for sex. I feel more than that. I feel tenderness, concern for you. It is real love. I thought last night that you felt it too."

"I just don't want you to expect too much. I am not a romantic. I can't afford to be."

"I don't expect it to last," she said sadly, "if that's what you mean."

"No. It won't last," he said morosely.

She forced a smile. "That doesn't mean that we don't love each other now. Love is not everlasting, whatever the poets say; it is the most fragile, gossamer, transitory thing imaginable. That is why it is beautiful. It is only a moment, or at most a season, almost a dream."

"Don't speak to me of love," he said roughly.

She was silent.

He paid the check. "I'll take you home."

He stood awkwardly inside the door of her room as if he were uncertain of his welcome. She walked away from him and stood looking out of the window across the busy intervening street at the red brick mass of the ancient Roman wall illuminated by the street lamps. He moved across the room and stood behind her. He touched her hair tentatively with his fingertips. At his touch, she turned away from the window and into his arms. Covering her face and neck with kisses he murmured, "I do love you. If ever I say I don't, I am a liar and a fool."

"I'll remember," she said softly, caressing him.

They lay together in the bed, her head resting

against his bare chest. He was still asleep. His chest rose and fell in a slow, regular rhythm. She pushed her body closer to his, feeling the warmth of his slightly convex stomach and the boney firmness of his thighs. He stirred. His eyes fluttered open. He looked into her face, faintly illuminated by the moonlight sifting through the translucent curtains at the window. He gently kissed her on the lips.

"What time is it?" he whispered.

"About four-thirty."

"An hour to daylight?"

"Yes. I hear a few birds already from the gardens outside the wall."

His lips sought her firm, warm skin. "You have a pretty, dark mole on this shoulder."

"Yes."

His lips brushed her. "And beautiful breasts."

She stroked his cheek with one hand as his mouth found one of her nipples. She began to breathe tremulously as his hands traveled down the small of her back and as they pressed against her buttocks she gave a deep sigh of surrender.

It was daylight when they awoke again. From the Borghese Gardens bird songs drifted to them on the cool morning air, audible in the hour between dawn and the beginning of heavy morning automobile traffic.

"You have a tiny scar on your forearm," she said, tracing it with a fingertip.

"I cut myself on a barbed-wire fence when I was a boy."

"What were you doing?" she asked lazily.

"Chasing my dog."

"What kind of dog?"

"A brown collie."

She stretched in his arms, arching her back and thrusting her breasts against him. "Let's drive into the country today."

"All right," he said after a slight hesitation. "I have to be back in the city by four."

She sensed the sudden tension in his body, but did not raise her eyes to look at him. "It is something unpleasant?"

"It is something I have to do."

"You cannot tell me about it? You might feel better sharing such things."

"It's a professional matter," he said shortly.

She lay in his arms a moment more without speaking further, but neither of them were now at ease. "I will take a shower," she said, getting up from the bed, "and you order breakfast." She tousled her hair with one hand as she moved toward the bathroom door. When she glanced around at him he was lying with his arms folded behind his head staring at the ceiling with a little frown of concentration between his eyes.

Lani sat alone in the small cafe sipping a campari. She did not appear surprised when a dark, slight man sat down beside her. She did not greet him and waited until the waiter had moved away to get his order before speaking.

"What have you learned?"

"The American has kept another appointment with Niesner."

Lani pursed her lips and gave an almost imperceptible assenting nod of her head. "This is the third time. It is more than a casual contact."

"What does it mean?"

"It suggests some sort of collaboration with Niesner. We do not yet know who Niesner is, but he is an enemy of Israel, of that we can be sure."

The slight man accepted his drink from the waiter's tray and sipped it with a frown on his face.

Lani carefully touched her lips with lipstick and snapped shut her red leather purse. She watched her companion finish his drink. "Follow Scott wherever he goes, except when he is with me. I'll always notify you when he leaves me so that you can resume contact."

The slight man leaned forward. "Only one thing worries me. The previous two times he has left the doctor's office, we lost him for a half hour. Do you suppose he suspects something?"

"I doubt it. You must be more alert. You'd better get back. We don't know how long he will be with Niesner."

After he left, she smoked a cigarette. Then she walked around the corner to a taxi stand.

Brune smiled at Scott. "How did it go?"

Scott lit a cigarette. "O.K., I guess. We had our usual friendly chat, then there was the same time lapse I experienced before. Judging by the clock, it was longer this time, nearly forty minutes."

"What was your reaction when your sense of time returned?"

"It was as if I had been inattentive, you know, where someone is talking to you and you are thinking of something else and suddenly you realize that all of this talk has been going on and you were unaware of it."

"Have you ever been under an anesthetic?"

"Yes."

"Was it like that? A slow return to consciousness, a murmur of voices, then sudden awareness?"

"No. It was like I say, more like your attention wandering and then coming back."

"You would say that your 'return' was instantaneous?"

"Yes." Scott lit another cigarette from the glowing stub of the cigarette in his hand.

Brune looked at him with the bright watchfulness of a curious bird. "Any after-effects?"

"No. Right afterward I felt a sense of relief, almost elation. Now I feel tired, a little nervous."

Brune nodded. "We must expect that. Now, I want you to relax and let your mind drift back to the moment you lost your time sense. Don't try too hard to recall, but starting at that point of time, do you remember anything?"

Scott stared in front of him. After a moment he bit his lip and then reluctantly shook his head. "No. Not a thing."

Brune turned away from him and picked up his pipe. "Don't worry about it," he said, filling the pipe. "Just let your mind play around the subject."

"O.K."

Sessena looked at Brune dourly, then walked over to a window and stared out of it over the rooftops.

After several moments Scott shook his head again. "Nothing," he said flatly.

"No dreams, emotions, tag-end reactions?" Brune insisted.

"No."

"How do you feel about this interview?"

"Feel about it?" Scott's voice was quizzical. "We agreed to do it, didn't we?"

"Does it annoy you?"

"Not particularly."

"How do you feel about me?"

Scott grinned. "You're a sweet kid."

Sessena gave a short hard laugh at the window, but did not turn around.

Brune was nettled. "These are really serious questions, Scott. They have a purpose."

"O.K. But I'm not over the hill, yet, if that's the angle you're interested in."

"I am sure you're not. If you were that susceptible we wouldn't have used you as our subject."

"Thanks, Brune," Scott said dryly. "You're all heart."

"That's all I have," Brune said crisply. He looked at Scott intently. "If you notice any delayed or secondary reactions, remember them for our next visit."

"Will do."

Sessena turned from the window and shook hands with Scott. "See you later, Scottie."

After Scott had gone, Sessena addressed Brune.

"How's he doing?"

"It's a little too early to tell. Right now he is merely undergoing hypnosis. Ideas are being planted in his subconscious. Too bad he can't give us some kind of clue about what goes on." Brune relit his pipe. "In time, Niesner will begin to direct him while under hypnosis, then the directions will be gradually replaced with radio electric stimuli. At least, that is what I surmise. Niesner, no doubt, has sophisticated methods I don't know about."

"What happens then?"

"That's about as far as Niesner got with Fenwick and Boad. I'm not sure whether he actually induced a state of hypnosis in them by radio waves and triggered pre-programmed reactions, or not. Fenwick's false reports on Israel from Bucharest suggest it, but perhaps Fenwick had his own personal reasons for those reports. Maybe he was just paid for them, like any avaricious human double agent."

"What about Boad?"

"If Boad killed the Israeli agent under radio-controlled orders, it was a triumph, an absolute triumph," Brune said enthusiastically. "Unfortunately, we don't know if that is true."

"Unfortunately," Sessena echoed.

"When we have reason to believe that Scott has reached the stage of programming, I'll put him in a state of hypnosis and try to debrief him. It's too early for that now. We don't want Niesner to notice our tampering. At this stage, he would recognize it at once."

"When you start hypnotizing Scott, won't that interfere with what Niesner is doing?"

"No. I will merely seek information. I'll be careful not to interject any hostile thoughts with respect to Niesner."

"Will we be able to tell if Scott becomes subservient to Niesner's will?"

"Not infallibly. We will have to observe. Of course,

I will help Scott maintain his equilibrium. He isn't entirely at Niesner's disposal, you know."

"He seems to think he can beat this thing, by the power of human will."

"It will have its effect," Brune spoke without conviction. "It will have its effect."

Scott felt tired and drained. He had completed his fifth session with Niesner followed by a long session alone with Brune. He had developed a dull headache. He ate a light supper in a small restaurant down a flight of stairs from a busy street whose name he afterward could not remember, bought a newspaper and a paperback book at a newsstand, and went to his room. He ordered a bottle of scotch, ice, and soda from room service and had slipped into his dressing gown when there was a light tap on the door. He opened it and found Lani Evron. She wore a simple white dress with a red leather belt matching the red ribbon that held back her hair.

"Come on in," he said, swinging the door wide, "I was expecting room service."

"Thank you." She entered the room and sat on a straight chair before a small desk, swinging one crossed leg and looking at him. "I expected to hear from you. Weren't we going to see a motion picture?"

"We did talk about it, Lani, but, really, I'm beat tonight. I thought I would have a drink and turn in early."

"No dinner?"

"I've already eaten."

"Oh. This is your night to be alone."

"I'm tired, sweetheart. That's all there is to it. I'd be bad company."

"Why are you tired? You weren't tired this afternoon."

"I just am." A hard rap came on the door. It was a waiter with his scotch, soda, and ice. "I'll mix you a drink," he said when they were alone again.

She sipped from her glass. "I'll run along in a minute," her tone was subdued.

"I'm sorry," he said. "I'll make it up tomorrow night."

"You assume I will be available."

"I hope you will. Christ, this is no personal rejection, Lani. I'm just not feeling well."

"Do you want a doctor?"

"No. It's nothing serious."

"I thought I might ask Doctor Niesner to make a house call."

They were like inanimate objects suspended in the silence of arrested time. At length the ice in his glass tinkled as he raised it to his lips. "So you have been following me?"

"I have had you followed."

He considered his glass. "Will it reassure you if I tell you that Niesner has nothing to do with you?"

.221.

"No."

"Or Israel?"

"I don't believe you. We both followed Fenwick's trail to Rome. Boad was a 'patient' of Niesner's. You must remember that I called on Niesner myself. He was not interested in me as a patient. Why is he interested in you?"

"There's no accounting for tastes." Scott tried to speak lightly.

She accepted another drink from him. "Why do you see this man?"

"I am taking treatment from him."

"Psychiatric treatment?" she asked unbelievingly.

"Yes."

"That's preposterous!"

He doggedly shook his head. "No, it isn't. I have been having a growing feeling of guilt about my role as a spy. I have fits of depression and melancholia. The doctor is helping me with this."

"What about Boad and Fenwick? We believe that Niesner is an Arab agent and was the control for Boad and Fenwick."

"Fenwick befriended Niesner as a refugee. He took Boad as a patient because Fenwick asked him to."

"And you?"

"I have the same problem as Boad."

"Guilt complex?"

"Yes."

"Americans are that fragile?"

"Some are."

"You are a hell of a liar, Mr. Scott."

He shrugged and drained his drink.

She got up to leave, but turned back to him at the door. "I love you, Bob. But I have my loyalties, too. You can't trust me if you work against my country."

"You're a good lover, but a loyal spy?"

"You can put it that way if you wish," she said evenly.

"I am not working against Israel and I love you too."

Her voice was low. "Don't lie to me, Bob, please don't."

"I won't lie, if you don't crowd me. I have my loyalties too."

She came over to him from the door and took his head between her hands. "We are both so damned noble. Why are we so damned noble, Bob?"

"We shouldn't have fallen in love," he said simply. "It's no good for us."

She kissed him. "I won't believe that until I must."

"Trust me on this one, Lani. It doesn't involve Israel. You don't risk divided loyalties."

"Can I believe you?" she said, looking into his eyes. "Can I believe you?"

He returned her searching gaze. "You can."

She kissed him again, long and tenderly.

"I shall see you tomorrow, dearest."

"It isn't wise for your team to go on shadowing me, you know. It may spoil what I am trying to do."

She spoke to him with one hand on the knob of the door leading into the hotel hallway. "I trust you, Robert Scott, but Israel doesn't." She blew him a kiss and was gone.

.19.

Scott was reluctant to enter the whitewashed room for his meeting with Brune. His seventh session with Dr. Neisner had left him with a feeling of peaceful lethargy. He didn't wish to subject himself to Brune's probing cross-examination. It had become highly irritating and somehow humiliating. On those occasions when Sessena was present, sitting to one side, silent, saturnine and noncommittal, even Sessena annoyed him. There was an attitude of suspended judgment in the room that in spite of himself made him feel defensive. He was doing this voluntarily, wasn't he? They all knew what they were about. Why was he being increasingly treated as an outsider? As if they had recently discovered some flaw in his character? He resented the looks exchanged between Brune and Sessena and the long silences. Undoubtedly they talked about him behind his back. He knew that Brune expected his personality to change; that was part of the challenge, but it hurt to have Sessena so clearly withhold his judgment. He had realized with a shock the preceding week that he was no longer informed about intelligence developments in his own area of Eastern Europe. Also, he did not know the new code. He had complained to Sessena who waved the objection away.

"Why should you be informed? You're on detached duty with enough on your hands as it is. Browne has taken over in Vienna for the time being. As for the code, it's changed periodically. You know that. You're only talking to Brune and me. You don't need the code for that."

Still, it rankled. They were selling him short. He needed an expression of their confidence in him. He desperately needed it.

Brune pushed a hand through his sandy hair and spoke cheerfully. "I'm glad Sessena is back in Rome for this one. We are going to try something a little different this time, Scott. Based on conscious observation after seven meetings you have little to tell us about Niesner's techniques at these sessions. Everything significant with Niesner is occurring on the subconscious level. That is where we must meet."

"What does that mean?" Scott asked shortly.

"It means that I must interrogate you under hypnosis."

Scott deeply inhaled his cigarette. "I don't know as I like the implication of that."

"There's no implication. You can't remember what happens at Niesner's during the time lapse, can you?"

"No," Scott said reluctantly, "probably because nothing happens. Personally, I think we're wrong about Niesner. He claims he is just a practicing psychiatrist and I've seen nothing to refute that."

"We know better, Scottie," Sessena interjected, speaking for the first time.

Scott shrugged. "O.K. Have it your way."

"I need your continued cooperation, Scott," Brune spoke quietly. "You've done magnificently. Now we must reach your subconscious. We need the information, but my contact with your subconscious will also help you to resist Niesner. That you can resist him and his mind-bending techniques is what you set out to prove, isn't it?"

"I am proving it."

"Will you cooperate with me?" Brune ignored Scott's assertion.

Scott puffed on his cigarette for a moment, an unhappy frown on his face. "O.K.," he said peevishly. "Let's get it over with."

"Is he under?" Sessena asked after a few minutes.

"Yes," Brune said quietly. "It wasn't too difficult. He is becoming very susceptible to hypnosis as a result of Doctor Niesner's therapy."

"He doesn't look hypnotized." Sessena's voice was doubtful.

"No. These new techniques are subtle. He will look and act natural even if Niesner turns him into a push-button spy."

Brune leaned toward Scott and spoke casually, but

incisively. "Scott, how do you feel about Doctor Niesner?"

"He is a very great man, a humanitarian."

"You would obey him?"

"It is not a question of obedience. He is my doctor and to recover my mental health, I wish to do as he prescribes."

"What if he asks you to do something wrong?"

"Wrong? Why would he do that? He is only prescribing for my health."

"I suggest that you must be very cautious about Dr. Niesner."

Scott's face clouded and he remained silent.

"Have you enemies?"

"I'm certain that I have," Scott said darkly. "I don't know who they are, that's all."

"What is Doctor Niesner's technique?"

"Technique?"

"How does he treat you?"

"He is very kind and understanding." Scott's voice became enthusiastic. "He has very gentle hands, sensitive fingers and a very warm voice and manner. We just talk about things that trouble me and I listen to soothing sounds."

"Music?"

"No. Just sounds. I like them."

"Can you describe them?"

Scott looked uncomfortable. "No. I can't. I don't

know what they are, but I like them. They are comforting."

"Like Dr. Niesner?"

"Yes. The sounds are like Dr. Niesner. That's what they are like."

"Do you feel loyal to the sounds?"

"Yes, I guess so."

"Would you do what they say?"

Scott wet his lips and his forehead became dotted with perspiration. "I don't know."

"You doubt that you should do what the sounds say?"

Scott nodded. "Doctor Niesner says that I should do what the sounds say, but . . ." his voice trailed off.

"Are you afraid to do what the sounds say?"

Scott wrung his hands and his face contorted. "I can't do what the sounds say," he spoke in a muffled voice. "I can't. I can't." He looked around wildly, half rising from his chair.

Brune gave him a glass of water, "Easy, old boy. Easy." He waited until Scott had drunk the water. "You don't need to do what the sounds say, Scott," Brune spoke soothingly. "Just let Doctor Niesner think that you will obey the sounds so that you won't hurt his feelings."

Scott nodded slowly, then his eyes sought Brune's. "You think I could do that? It would be all right?"

"Of course. It's the only thing to do. As a free man

you can't obey sounds. Doctor Neisner doesn't understand this. You and I understand this."

"What if he finds out that I am pretending?" Scott asked apprehensively.

"He won't," Brune's voice was firm and incisive. "You must remember," he added gently, "that we weren't going to tell Dr. Niesner everything, no matter how much we liked him."

"Yes. I remember that."

"It's all right to like Doctor Niesner and to do what he says in his office, but you must not obey the sounds."

"No. I must not."

"You can pretend to obey."

"Yes. I can pretend."

Scott rubbed his damp forehead. "Was I under?"

"Yes."

"How long?"

"Fifteen minutes. Then I brought you out."

Scott forced a grin. "What's the verdict? Am I a zombie?"

"Of course not," Brune said reassuringly. "You are doing very, very well in a unique situation."

"That's good." Scott shook a cigarette out of a pack and placed it between his lips with fingers that trembled slightly. "Does anyone have a drink? I really feel done in."

Sessena poured two inches of scotch into a glass from a pocket flask and handed it to him.

Scott took a draught from the glass. He coughed and winked at Sessena. "That's better."

He slowly sipped the rest of the scotch. "What did you learn?"

Brune considered. "You have developed a subconscious loyalty to Niesner. He is now trying to program you for radio-controlled response. You are resisting that."

"I sure as hell hope so."

"I think you will."

"I think I will, too, Brune," Scott's tone was positive. "That's the name of the game."

"Tell me, have you had any sense of a time lapse other than in Niesner's office?"

"No," Scott said slowly, looking at him.

"If you do, will you let me know at once?"

"Sure. Even if my watch stops it will scare hell out of me." He stretched and yawned. "My God. I'm pooped."

"Go on home, Scottie. Forget it and have a good night's rest," Sessena said gruffly.

"I think I'll just do that. O.K., Brune?"

"O.K., old boy. This is going according to form. Don't worry about it."

When Scott had gone, Sessena sat down heavily on one of the straight chairs and lit a cigarette. "That's one of the damnest things I ever saw or heard."

"Damned is right. It's Mephistopheles and Faust in real life."

"Has Niesner really got him, Brune?"

"No. Not yet. He is resisting the idea of hypnosis induced by radio and control by radio signals. That is the crux of the whole problem. When he arrived here he was under considerable subconscious strain about those radio sounds. I resolved that for him under hypnosis. You noticed how relieved and relaxed he was afterward?"

"Do you think he can pretend to obey the radio sounds to satisfy Niesner and still remain his own man?"

"I don't know," Brune said simply.

"Can we tell which way it goes?"

"I hope so, but we are dealing with pretty delicate stuff. Brain waves, memory, personality. We don't know where it can lead and neither does Niesner. However, he has his guinea pig."

"And so do we," Sessena said bitterly.

"Our motives are different," Brune said defensively.

"Are they?" Sessena glared at him. "I'd say we are peas from the same pod. The only human being around here is the victim."

"He's not a victim. He's a hero, like the men who submitted to yellow fever experiments in Cuba at the turn of the century."

"Let's hope that's how it turns out. It's a tug of war now for sure. He'll either be our man or theirs."

"Not necessarily," Brune said somberly. "We could both lose him to madness or suicide."

Sessena's eyes jerked up to Brune's and he savagely ground out his cigarette. "I'm leaving Rome for a few days and looking forward to it. Let's get the hell out of here."

The light breeze billowed out the curtain and filled the room with scented night air. Lani awoke, chilled and aware that she was alone in the big soft bed. She lifted herself on one elbow and looked across the room. A figure was sitting quietly in a slipper chair by the window.

"Darling?"

"Yes," Scott answered.

"Is something the matter?"

"I can't sleep. I thought I would sit up for awhile."

She sat up on the edge of the bed and after pushing her feet into blue satin mules, slipped into a thin dressing gown of blue satin and lace. Dropping down on an embroidered hassock beside his chair, she threw her unpinned hair back on her shoulders and took both of his hands in hers.

They sat silently together this way for an extended length of time. He cleared his throat once or twice, but did not speak. She thought of the two weeks that had passed since she had accused him of seeing Niesner. For three days thereafter they had not seen one another. When they had met again, by accident in a neighborhood drugstore, their manner had been tentative, almost shy. They had gone, at his invitation, to the Ambassciatori Bar and as his hand had closed firmly over hers under the table in an intimate corner, an almost overwhelming surge of physical desire had swept over them both. They had known then that they desperately needed each other and that they could only stay together if they ignored the outside influence seeking to pull them apart.

Now their relationship was even more intensely personal than before. What little conversation they made was about trivia. Their happiness was flawed, but they laughed more than ever. Lightheartedness was almost an article of faith, faith that all was normal, that all would be well. Nevertheless, she was deeply concerned about Scott. He was as tanned, as relaxed, and as amicable as ever, but she knew that it was not natural, as before. It was a carefully, even painfully, maintained pose.

She associated the change with Dr. Niesner, but she did not know why. Scott was playing some terrible game with Niesner. It did not involve Israel, of that she was now sure. Her love for Scott gave her an intuitive feeling about his attitudes. He was not a devious nor a complicated man. It was his characteristic American simplicity that endeared him to her. He was not making love to her and plotting with Niesner against Israel. Israeli intelligence reluctantly took her word for this though they ordered her to continue to stay close to him. On one or two occasions she tried to speak to Scott about Niesner, but he immediately turned on her angrily and for several hours thereafter was aloof and cool toward her. She learned that it was better to avoid the subject.

He spoke into the night. "You know I love you, Lani?"

"Yes. I know that."

He shifted uneasily in the chair. "I *do* love you." His voice was hoarse.

She lifted her lips to him and brushed his cheek with her lips.

"I love you," he said almost convulsively, grasping both of her upper arms through her negligee. "I love you."

His fingers probed into her flesh. "You are hurting me," she gasped.

He stared at her almost uncomprehendingly for a moment, a dew of perspiration on his face, then he released her with a dry sob and buried his face in his hands.

"You'd better leave," he muttered.

"No, darling, I won't. You need me."

"It's not safe for you." Then he added in anguish, "God help me."

"Don't be foolish," she said matter of factly. "You wouldn't hurt me."

He seized her hands. "No. I wouldn't hurt you. You know that, don't you?"

"Of course I know that."

He sat silently in the chair, spent and shaking. "I think I have control now," his voice was far away.

"Wouldn't you like to discuss this with me, dearest? Wouldn't it help?"

"I can't discuss it with anyone. I am in this alone. I am all alone to the end, to the very end."

"I love you. I could help if you would let me." She looked at him imploringly.

"No. This is between him and me."

"Him?"

He was silent. "Let's go back to bed," he said flatly, after an interval.

He awoke at dawn with all of the tension gone from his body. He stretched and lay looking in a dreamlike languor at the circular design in bas-relief around the light fixture. In his half-reverie it was sometime before he remembered that Lani had been with him earlier in the night. She was gone now. He vaguely recalled that they had had an argument. He dozed off and awoke again with the room bathed in early morning sunlight. He swung out of bed and reached for his bathrobe on a nearby chair, wincing as he did so. He held his hands out and stared uncomprehendingly at the bruised and split knuckles. There were several long scratches down one forearm. Shaking his head groggily he started for the bathroom. As he rounded the corner of the bed he noticed a body lying in a crumpled heap in a corner of the room nearest the hallway door. He approached it with a cold, shrinking sensation. He knew before he turned the bloody face toward him that it was Lani.

.20.

He ran into the bathroom to get a wet towel and had to retch into the toilet before he could return to the bedroom. He wiped her face moaning, "What have I done? Good God! What have I done?" Lifting her body he laid her on the bed and clumsily felt for her pulse. It was faint and erratic. He lifted the telephone receiver with a shaking hand.

"*Si?*"

"There's a badly hurt woman in this room. Please call for an emergency ambulance. We must get her to a hospital at once."

"Right away, sir, 208."

"For God's sake, hurry!"

"Right away, sir." The line crackled and then buzzed in his ear.

He drew up a chair and sat dumbly holding one of Lani's inert hands until a doctor and two orderlies arrived. Before Lani had been removed, the police arrived and he was arrested.

He sat dejectedly in a whitewashed room with Brune and Sessena.

"She will recover, Scott," Brune said. "She looked in worse shape than she was. You gave her a proper beating, but no permanent damage. The concussion was a problem for a day or so, but she's conscious now."

Scott nodded. "I don't even remember it," he said hopelessly. "How could I have done such a thing?"

"Niesner ordered you to do it. It was the kind of test he would use about now, an assault contrary to your true instincts."

"Oh, my God, my God," Scott moaned. "I've become a zombie."

"We will have to intensify our own efforts through hypnosis to counteract Niesner's influence. We obviously have underestimated the intensity of his therapy." Brune said, glancing at Sessena. "We also overestimated the subject's capacity to resist."

"Yes. I thought I had a soul," Scott said in desolate tones, pausing after each word.

"Let's forget the theology and the scientific doubletalk," Sessena said impatiently. "If we can't keep Scottie free of this radio control bit, we've lost the game. He'll have to break off contact with Niesner."

"We haven't lost the game, Sessena," Brune said easily. "Scott isn't under complete control or he wouldn't accept responsibility for his acts or show remorse. I really think Niesner made a mistake with this test. I think he underestimated Scott's attachment to this woman."

"I love her," Scott muttered.

Brune glanced at Sessena significantly.

"Whatever we do on the mind bending bit," Sessena

said, "our immediate problem is moving Scott out of Italy. That's why I rushed back here from London. We had one hell of a time prying him out of the hands of the Italian police. Fortunately, the woman refused to press charges when she regained consciousness. Also, we claimed diplomatic immunity."

"Can I see her?" Scott asked quietly.

"No," Sessena said shortly. He lit a cigarette. "You're flying to Vienna tonight. We'll be on the same plane in case you get into trouble. Otherwise, we won't give you a tumble."

"What do I say to Niesner?"

"Drop him a postcard."

"He has an office in Vienna, Scott," Brune interjected. "He'll contact you there. You're too valuable to him now to let you get away like Boad or Fenwick. If he doesn't contact you, you can contact him after we have shored up your personality a bit."

"What will he think?" Scott asked with a worried frown.

"He will think you broke and ran after his test and he will be curious about what went wrong. You needn't worry, I think we have Niesner hooked."

"What am I going to do in Vienna?" Scott asked Sessena.

"You'll go to your apartment and to your office in the Embassy as if nothing had happened. We'll improvise from there."

"As if nothing had happened," Scott repeated bitterly. He glanced up. "I have no official duties, I suppose?"

"None except this big one, Scottie, but no one will know that other than Browne, Brune, and me."

"Not even the Ambassador?"

"Not even the Ambassador."

"What happens next?"

Sessena handed him an envelope. "You go to the airport. The Embassy paid your hotel bill and will send on your gear. Happy flying."

Vienna, even in spring, suited Scott's somber mood more than Rome. Rome is burnt ochre under a clear blue sky, filled with flowers and vibrant with an excess of life. Vienna is somber gray and pale yellow muted under overcast skies where life has a quality of melancholy resignation. Rome is loud and tumultuous. It has learned nothing from its long history. Vienna has learned everything and contemplates its present with an air of pensive detachment.

Scott's apartment was stuffy when he entered it. He threw open a casement window toward the west and let the cool air of evening flow in. The sun had broken through banks of clouds just as it touched the horizon and bathed the city in a golden twilight. The room in which he sat was warm and bright for a brief period and then as the sun slipped below the horizon became gloomy, shrouded in the dusk.

Scott turned on all of the lights with a shiver and

walked out to the small kitchen to brew a pot of coffee.

He forced himself to read an historical novel until he felt sleepy. To his surprise, when he went to bed he fell at once into a deep dreamless sleep that lasted until morning.

Browne looked at him curiously when he appeared at the Embassy. "You look thinner, Scott. I thought detached duty in Rome would agree with you."

"It was detached and strenuous."

"You may like the next spot better." He handed him a card with an address on it.

"Attersee?"

"Be there tonight, the boss man said. Drive one of our government-issue automobiles. See upper Austria."

Scott shrugged. "I might as well go now."

"Why not? You're footloose and fancy-free. Let me know sometime how you get these assignments. I'm usually photographing dog-eared files in dusty archives."

He drove to Attersee and the Salzkammergut through a sunlit, green world of small country villages and verdant fields, but his thoughts turned inward and were bleak and sere. His assault on Lani had destroyed his self-respect and since he did not even remember the episode he felt a fearful weakening of his sense of personal identity. What was he? He kept asking himself. Could all of the things he had assumed about himself since his first sense of self-awareness be untrue? Was he not the second son of a family of English origin that

.241.

had lived in Indiana for four generations? Did he not resemble his maternal grandfather? Was not his temperament like his father's? He had always been told so. Hadn't he been reared according to certain family and community standards? Was he not honest, loyal, steadfast? Did he not feel a sense of gallantry toward women? Was he not, in short, Bob Scott from Valparaiso, Indiana? Unique, separate, identifiable even among the billions of human beings on earth?

But he had beaten a woman until she was nearly dead. A woman he loved. Brune said he did it on radio orders from Niesner in a state of carefully controlled hypnosis. Was he still Bob Scott? Or in those time lapses with Niesner had he cooperated in destroying his own identity? Was he Faust and Niesner his Mephistopheles? His palms were wet on the steering gear and he wiped them one after another on a handkerchief.

And what of his immortal soul and his personal responsibility for sin? He had been reared as a Christian and an Episcopalian. If Niesner could control his actions at will, what of his soul? Had it been destroyed? Had it left him? Was he now alone in a dark, Godless universe?

He began to shiver uncontrollably and stopped by an inn on the edge of a village he had just passed through. He parked the automobile on the dusty shoulder of the road and entered the dark public room. It was redolent with the odors of wood smoke, beer, and cooking. A heavyset woman came forward, wiping her hands on her apron, and smiled at him.

"*Grüss Gott.*"

"*Grüss Gott.* May I have a stein of beer?"

"*Natürlich.* It is a nice day. Would you like to sit out-of-doors?" She gestured toward a side door.

"*Ja, danke.*" He walked through the door onto a wooden balcony with a thick rustic wooden railing consisting of sturdy palings alternating with decorative wooden cutouts of squirrels, deer, rabbits, and the forest implements of human beings—walking pikes, Tyrolean hats, and crossed guns. The balcony was in full sun. He sat down at a rough hewn table and looked out over the green fields and orchards that extended in undulating waves until they blended with the misty foothills of the alps in the south. It was so beautiful that he was almost overcome by his sense of personal despair.

The heavyset woman came out on the balcony, her face wreathed in smiles. In addition to the foaming dark stein of beer, she had a plate with two slices of thick buttered bread and several fresh green scallions. "I thought that you might be hungry as well as thirsty, *mein Herr.*"

"*Danke shoen,*" Scott said gratefully and looking into the pleasant, plain face, returned her smile.

"*Ja.* You will feel better," she said in a motherly way. "Something to eat in the sunshine, it puts things right again." She stood, her hands clasped under her apron. "You have a good afternoon for a drive. Go slowly, see the countryside."

"I am driving to Attersee."

"*Ach,* Attersee! It is a beautiful lake. You stay with friends?"

"Yes. It is a villa, I think."

"Ah, *ja,* a villa. There are lovely villas there." She nodded and smiled, then turned to go. "Eat and drink in good health."

The smile remained on Scott's face after she had left. This simple, kindly human contact had steadied his nerves. He felt the warmth of the sun, the softness of the spring breeze. It was not a dark Godless universe. He was not alone. He was a human being with his spark of the divine spirit and for the first time he began to realize what the theologians meant.

The way along the lake to the villa was a narrow, high crowned road covered with a fine beige gravel. Heavily pruned linden trees were planted on each side and formed a formal green file along which he drove until he turned into a driveway marked by two pillars of field stone. A wooden slab was fastened to one of them with the words *Villa au Lac* burned into it.

Sessena was waiting for him at the rear entrance having heard the sound of the tires on the gravel. "You made it in good time."

"Yes. I enjoyed the drive."

Sessena looked at him more closely. "I think you're back in charge, Scottie."

.244.

Scott grinned. "I think I am, Ernie."

Sessena took him by his free arm as he carried his bag into the house. "I didn't think a Hoosier boy would let a Kraut head shrinker get him down for very long."

"Where's Brune?"

"He'll be along. We three are going to batch it here until we are sure you are on top of this thing."

"Who's going to cook?"

"I'll give you plain home cooking out of cans."

"I feel honored, but worried."

Sessena punched him playfully on the upper arm.

They were playing two-handed bridge before a fire in the large living room when Brune arrived.

"Nice place," he said, rocking back and forth on his heels, his hands thrust deeply into his pockets as he looked out of a window overlooking the lake. "I like the green lawn reaching down to the water."

"It belongs to a well-heeled Central European who cooperates with us for a variety of complex reasons," Sessena said.

"Very nice." He turned around to Scott. "I'm glad to see that you are over the shock of your experience, Scott. We are isolated in these pleasant surroundings in order to concentrate on our problem in security and without interruption. You and I are going to spend several hours alone each day unraveling what Niesner has done to you. The purpose is to free you from a mental condition where you react to radio-induced

.245.

hypnosis and to hypnotic suggestion given to you previously. Physical and mental lassitude is our goal."

Scott nodded.

Brune brought his hands together with a gentle slap. "Good. One thing I've sensed throughout is an antagonism on your part. It has been an obstruction. Since your experience the other night, I believe you are now willing to admit that you need my help."

"Yes," Scott said quietly.

"Very well," Brune smiled. "I may seem rather clinically detached and impersonal, but you have no doubt that our interests are identical?"

"None."

"After our supper, we'll begin. There is no time to lose. We must have you back in your apartment in five days' time. You will be under my hypnosis for an hour or so at a time, several times a day. It will be physically exhausting and nervously debilitating, but we should get results. Between our sessions together I want you to relax completely, sun yourself, swim, row on the lake, but you are not to read, and you definitely must not listen to music. We will disconnect the radio as a precaution."

"I understand."

"Good. You will see that it will work out all around. You haven't subjected yourself to this ordeal for nothing. I will learn much about Niesner's techniques and you will regain control of your mental processes. When that is done, Sessena can send you back to Vienna prepared to function as a double agent. Everybody will be happy."

Scott looked at him. "I believe you mean that."

"I wouldn't say it if I didn't."

.21.

Brune was right. He did have a feeling of physical and mental lassitude at Attersee. But it was not unpleasant for it was accompanied by a shedding of care and responsibility. In Rome, with Niesner, he had been faced by an adversary with the results unknown. Here at Attersee he knew the worst. He was a patient in Brune's hands. He could relax. He was among friends. He had no responsibility at all. He sat down in a pleasant upstairs room alone with Brune and relaxed under the benign therapy of hypnosis. As with Niesner he had no sense of elapsed time during hypnosis. He did feel an acute sense of fatigue afterward as he became aware of time and aware that Brune was smiling at him, several pages of new notes on the small table beside him.

He liked best rowing out on the smooth lake and lying back on the air cushions on the stern thwart, as the boat, oars boated, drifted down the lake with the almost imperceptible current and the wind. The sky was a vivid blue with a few soft white clouds. At the periphery of his vision he could sense, rather than see, the green forests covering the hills that surrounded the lake. There was an almost complete absence of the conventional sounds of civilization; outboard motors, airplanes, human shouts and cries, amplified music or voices. He would hear the soft plop of a fish as it fell back into the water after throwing itself into the air to catch an insect, the sound of oarlocks as some never to be known stranger rowed by at a distance, the distant throb of the motors of the white double-decked lake steamer growing louder as it passed by him several hundred feet offshore, but still impersonal and disembodied, a congenial sound in a peaceful world. The wake from the steamer would shortly thereafter reach the rowboat causing it to roll and pitch momentarily, the half inch or so of water beneath the slatted floorboards sloshing back and forth.

Sometimes the boat would drift inshore and he would find himself looking up into the branches of a fully leafed tree, the sky merely a blue backdrop to a dancing myriad of green leaves. He would lean over the side of the boat, staring down into the cold, clear water, seeing the brown lake bottom a meter or less beneath the surface, covered with the sodden brown leaves of the tree's previous year. He was reminded at such times of his boyhood when there were no decisions, no responsibilities, and all of the important things to be done, the tests to be withstood, were awaiting in a far off, limitless future. The sheer abundance of time, as he then conceived it, promoted tranquility and ease. It was enough to contemplate the magic of the present moment, to develop a sensual awareness of

.250.

muted sounds, the movements of nature, to feel sun and air on one's skin.

He found time at Attersee to do what he had done twenty years before in Indiana; to examine a leaf and to dissect it with a thumbnail edging along the strong fibers, cutting into the green juicy pulp until it filled the space between finger and nail; to weigh a stone, to imagine the Paleozoic pressures that formed it and then to send it skipping across the smooth lake surface until it lost momentum and sank from sight. Dragonflies would land on the end of his oars as he rested while rowing back to the villa, touching down lightly on the wet tip ends, preening in the sunlight, creating their iridescent shimmer, and then gracefully rising into the warm afternoon air as he slowly dipped the oar into the water again, reluctantly taking another of the strokes that propelled him homeward.

He would secure the boat by a single weathered rope through an iron ring attached to the short wooden dock that extended into the water from a moss-covered stone retaining wall. His bare feet would leave the rough warmth of the wooden planks of the dock and sink into the moist coolness of the green lawn grasses as he walked toward the stone and frame house where Brune waited in the upstairs room.

He gained self-confidence each day as the vague tensions which had beset him in Rome subsided. He felt that he had again a unity of spirit, a oneness, a sense of identity that had been slipping away from him.

"I think you are ready to return to Vienna," Brune said on the evening of the fifth day. "Niesner had thrown you badly off balance. I have to admire the way in which he built upon your past experiences and your desires, to create a new personality which would function in a very narrow range of your total psyche. He was successful because he did not seek to destroy anything that was there, only to divert it toward his purposes."

"I never had a desire to beat a woman," Scott objected.

"No, but you engaged in hand-to-hand combat in Vietnam. He merely suggested to you that the young woman you beat was an enemy threatening you with physical attack. If he wanted you to steal important documentation, for example, he would convince you under hypnosis that you were merely saving the documents from a fire. Everything you would do for him would be compatible with your training and moral code. Only your motivation would be false."

"And now?"

"Now you understand under hypnosis what he really wants of you, but you will dissemble and pretend to do what he wishes."

"Will he realize that is what I am doing?"

"He might, but I think that he is too sure of himself,

.252.

too arrogant to suspect that anyone could master his method and use it against him."

Scott turned to Sessena. "What do I do in Vienna?"

"You will resume your normal duties. Wait twenty-four hours, then call Niesner's Vienna office for an appointment. Play it along from there. I think he will try to test you again and then he may reveal how he plans to use you. Brune and I will move into a command post in a house out in Heitzing. We will be there if you need us, but you are now on your own. Brune has finished his work. He has learned through you what he wanted to know about Niesner's techniques in mind bending and he has given you, through hypnotic counter-suggestion, the support you need to withstand Niesner. Your work and my work is just beginning, however. You have to encourage Niesner to use you as a counterspy. Then we'll use you to feed misinformation to the Russians and to penetrate their apparatus."

Scott lit a cigarette. "I'm glad we are getting back to specifics. These trips I've been taking into the metaphysical world have been wearing."

"The specific is always a comfort," Sessena grinned.

Scott drove back to Vienna in a steady rain the following morning and entered the familiar office in the Embassy shortly after noon. He was filled with a feeling of excitement and anticipation at a renewal of contact with Niesner and concentrated on his routine intelligence responsibilities with difficulty. He had beer, sausage, and black bread alone at a small nearby restaurant, went to a motion picture and was in bed by ten o'clock.

Early the next afternoon he reached for the telephone book and found Niesner's office number. After dialing, the sound of ringing was repeated eight or nine times without a response. He hung up with a sensation of intense disappointment. He tried again at hour intervals and at seven o'clock a woman's voice responded. *"Bitte?"*

"Is this the office of Doctor Anton Niesner?"

"Yes."

"I am a patient of Doctor Niesner's. He was treating me in Rome. However, I have now returned to Vienna and I would like to resume my treatment here."

"Your name, please?"

"Scott. Robert Scott."

"One moment please." In three or four minutes the voice was back on the line.

"Thank you for waiting, Mr. Scott. Doctor Niesner will be in Vienna tomorrow. His regular schedule is completely booked, but he could see you tomorrow evening about eight P.M. Unfortunately, he must return to Rome the next day and he will not be back in Vienna until the first of next week."

"Eight P.M. will be fine."

"You have the address?"

"No." She gave him a street and apartment number near Karlskirche and hung up.

By nightfall the next day a cold rain which had

begun tentatively about midafternoon following a gray, humid, overcast morning had become a steady downpour.

Scott turned up the collar of his raincoat as he stepped from the taxicab and hurried across the worn sidewalk, dodging the puddles which had collected on its uneven surface and also the cascade of water plunging down beside the apartment building door from an overflowing eave. Inside the lobby of the building he stomped his feet on the marble floor and shook the water from his hat as he smiled at the concierge in his small cubicle. "Miserable weather."

"*Ja.*"

"I have an appointment with Doctor Niesner."

The concierge peered at a paper before him and then indicated an elevator consisting of a worn metal cage. "Fourth floor."

Niesner's Vienna office was a comfortable old apartment with high ceilings, massive furniture, and heavy velvet draperies. Scott had spent only a brief interval in a small parlor before he was led into the long salon by a slight dark, middle-aged woman who then disappeared. The draperies were closed, shutting out the sounds of the storm outside. The porcelain stove in the corner had a small fire laid in it despite the lateness of the season and radiated an unwanted heat that made the air heavy and oppressive.

The subdued lighting from lamps on several tables, the rows of books against the walls, the thick carpets, all contributed to Scott's impression that this room had been conceived to create a world of its own to exclude or at least to muffle all outside influences. It was in startling contrast to the room in the modern building overlooking Rome where he had met Niesner before.

He was not aware that Niesner had entered the room until he spoke behind him. "The surroundings are somewhat different, aren't they, Mr. Scott," he said pleasantly, sensing Scott's thoughts.

"Yes, though charming."

"Not charming, Viennese, yes, but I never think of Vienna as charming. Vienna goes much deeper than that. It has a certain silken hold on life. It enslaves one, smothers one in excess even as one futilely hopes to break away. Vienna is like a beautiful, beguiling woman, arch, coquettish, radiating a heavy perfume, expensive, demanding, possibly ruinous. It is no wonder that Viennese like to leave their city for a simple holiday in the countryside. She becomes too much to endure, a surfeit of elegant coyness, so to speak." He walked over to the windows and drawing back the draperies opened the casement windows. The rain fell straight past the windows in wet gray sheets and no air stirred, yet the room immediately seemed less oppressive.

"However," Niesner continued, turning from the windows with a smile, "I am Viennese enough to enjoy these surroundings and my patients rather expect it. After all, Freud was Viennese. Psychoanalysis began in an environment like this." He gestured toward a chair. "Sit here, Mr. Scott. The thread of our relationship has been interrupted and we must make a special effort to reestablish our rapport." He smiled in gentle reproof.

"I had a terrifying experience in Rome. I am afraid that I ran away."

"And what was this experience?"

"I badly beat the Israeli woman with whom I was having an affair."

Niesner's expression was noncommittal. "Were you jealous?"

"No. I had no motivation."

"There is always a motivation for violent action, Mr. Scott, ranging from calculated premeditation to spontaneous anger."

"I had nothing against her," Scott said morosely. "I don't even remember doing it or why it was. That is why I was so frightened."

"You should have come to me. I am your doctor."

"All I could think about was leaving Rome. I came back here."

"And what happened to the woman?"

"I don't know. The Embassy was going to take care of her and hush things up, since I am an intelligence officer."

"I see. And won't your colleagues be concerned about this outburst?"

"They sure will. That worries me too."

Niesner was silent for a moment. "And how have you passed the time during the past week?"

"I stayed in the Salzkammergut until I had better control of myself."

"With friends?"

"No. I moved about to a different place each night under an assumed name. I didn't want to be found."

Niesner looked at him searchingly. "It seems to have agreed with you."

"Yes, I feel better, but I am more convinced than ever that I need psychiatric help. Will I have another of these irrational outbursts, doctor?"

"I rather think not," Niesner's tone of voice suggested that he had some reservations. "As a matter of fact, we might find that this violent outburst of yours helped your condition by removing a wayward element of suppressed emotion. What I have been seeking for through hypnosis, Mr. Scott, is that element in your personality which you are trying to deny."

"You think that I am a violent man?"

"No more than any other. There is some brute in all of us. It is not wise to be too civilized, you know. That is what I was trying to suggest to you about Vienna. Freud sometimes thought that the entire city needed psychoanalysis."

"That makes me feel better, somehow, though I don't suppose it has a direct application to me."

"You are engaged in espionage. The problem is just more acute for you because you operate outside the conventional confines of society, but it is essentially the same problem."

Niesner put the tips of his fingers together in a prayer-like gesture and looked at Scott over them. "Now I think we should proceed with our hypnotic therapy. We will know more about the dimensions of our problem after that."

The time lapse was more than two hours. Scott's wristwatch indicated twenty minutes to eleven. He had a dull headache and felt mentally drained. Niesner had turned from him and was staring out of the window. In the lamplight his profile looked stern. Scott lit a cigarette and waited, his palms moist.

Niesner turned toward Scott. "On the whole," he said lowly, "I think we can proceed. You do need some intensive therapy, however. I feel that we are not quite where we were in Rome. Your problem is somewhat more complicated."

"You mean I am more ill than before?"

"No. We can't qualify this problem in quite that way. Your experience with the woman, your flight from Rome to Vienna, the lapse in your treatments have all changed the circumstances of your case. It may be for the better or for the worse. At the moment I cannot say which. I think, Mr. Scott," he added carefully, "That I owe it to you as your doctor to remain in Vienna an extra day or so to treat you. This is a critical moment for you."

"I'd be very grateful," Scott said humbly, "but what of your patients in Rome?"

"No problem," Niesner waved his hand. "We shall reschedule my appointments. I shall do a little more in Vienna sooner and a little less in Rome until later. It is rather like rescheduling optional surgery in order to handle emergency surgery."

"I am an emergency?"

"I overstated the comparison, but I do wish to see you for several hours tomorrow and the following day."

Scott wet his dry lips and forced a smile. "Whatever you say, Doctor."

.22.

The next forty-eight hours were an exhausting ordeal for Scott. As usual, he could not recall any part of the hours he spent under hypnosis, but he could recognize the now familiar mental and physical fatigue and the depressing sense of the infliction of an outrage against his person that remained with him after his sessions with Niesner were over. In the late afternoon of the second day, Niesner seemed satisfied. He was returning to Rome the next morning. He gave Scott an appointment in Vienna three days later.

Scott returned to his apartment and mixed himself a solitary drink. He sank into an upholstered chair and laid his head back against the cushions. If only there was not so much of this, the most important part, that he could not remember. Niesner seemed satisfied. Did this mean that Brune had failed? Was he now again subject to unnatural orders from Niesner? A dew of perspiration broke out on his forehead. Surely his will was in the scale too? Even though he could not remember, surely he was not reduced to a mental jelly, his brain nothing more than a battleground for Niesner and Brune? He rubbed his eyes with the back of his hand and arose to fix another drink. After mixing it he stared into the mirror behind his little bar at his fatigued face. If Niesner had suspected that Brune was interfering with Niesner's programming of his responses under hypnosis, would he have returned to Rome? Would he not have appeared agitated? Instead he had maintained his usual clinical aplomb and professional detachment. Then, didn't this mean that he had performed well under hypnosis? That he was still his own man? The thought made him feel better. He ought to eat something, but he wasn't hungry. He sat down with his new drink and put his feet up on a worn leather hassock.

The tap on his door was so light that if he had not been sitting silently, staring at the bubbles slowly rising to the top of his glass from the ice cubes, he would not have heard it. He laid his glass on the glass counter of the bar in passing and opened it.

A voice spoke from the shadows of the hallway. "May I come in?" It was Lani Evron.

He opened the door wider so that she could pass. She stopped inside the room and turned to look at him. "Aren't you going to shut the door?" she asked softly.

"Yes, of course." He slowly pushed it until it caught in its latch with an audible click.

"What is that?" She indicated his glass.

"Scotch and soda."

"I shall have one, too."

He mixed the drink and handed it to her. She sat down in a chair with one leg folded under her in an attitude so familiar that he yearned to take her in his arms, to beg her forgiveness, to cover her face with kisses.

"How have you been?" She asked.

"Busy. Terribly busy." He hesitated. "I suppose I should ask how you are."

"Yes, you might."

He sat down across from her. "Will you believe me if I say how sorry I am?"

She ignored his question. "I have recovered. A few bruises still require makeup, but they will disappear in a few days' time. That is in the past. I am not concerned with the past." Her eyes met his searchingly as she sipped her drink. "Why did you run away?"

He cleared his throat. "I don't know. I was afraid."

"You aren't the kind of man who runs away . . . or beats women."

"I did both." His voice was barely audible.

"Someone ordered you away from Rome. Who was it?"

"No one."

"I don't believe you."

He looked at her defiantly. "I don't give a damn if you do or not."

"You don't remember beating me, do you?"

"Yes, I do."

"Where was I when you first hit me? What did I say?"

He was silent.

"You do not remember."

.263.

"I have tried to forget about it."

"You never knew what you did, *neshomeleh*. You forget that I was there, the person most intimately involved."

"I'd rather not talk about it."

"You can't talk about it, you see? But I can. We were in bed together. You had been making love to me. You forget how intimately I had come to know you in the weeks just past. I am a woman and you had been my lover; don't you think I could sense your every mood? Lying beside me, you suddenly became rigid, then you relaxed and became rigid again. I said to you, 'Bob! What is it?' I switched on the light by the bed and you turned to me with a look of anguish on your face which I shall never, never forget. You tried to speak, a spasm twisted your face, and then you cried, 'My God. Oh, my God,' in the most beseeching, the most desolate voice I have ever heard. In a moment you were calm again, but you had become a different person. You laid on your side, facing me as if you were waiting for something, then your eyes fixed me with a glittering look of utter hatred, but they weren't your eyes at all, don't you see? You weren't there any more." She stopped, and fishing a cigarette out of her handbag lit it. She inhaled deeply before continuing in a low voice. "I was suddenly afraid for my life. It was an instinct for self-preservation. I tried to get out of bed, but you seized my arm in a hard, cruel grip and pulled me back. Then you struck me."

She looked across the room at Scott from dark, wet eyes. "I won't go into the details. Besides, it was not long until I became unconscious."

Scott had covered his face with his hands as she talked. He spoke through them in a muffled voice. "I'm not accountable, Lani. Can't you understand that? I go to Doctor Niesner because I need psychiatric help."

She slowly shook her head. "You know that I have not believed that for a very long time. You forget that I shared your bed in Rome and sensed the change in you after you began to visit Doctor Niesner. This man has some hold over you. He is turning you against me as he turned Fenwick and Boad against Israel. I will not let him do this to you."

"Very dramatic," he said in a thick voice, "but I don't want you around. I don't need a foreign agent in my bedroom. I have a job to do. I'm not going to let an Israeli whore hang around my neck and keep me from doing it."

Lani's face paled and her hands closed tightly over one another in her lap, but she did not speak.

"Do you understand that?"

"I hear you," she said in a low voice.

"What I do with Niesner or what he does with me is my business; no part of it is your business. I don't need you. I don't want you around. Understand?" His voice rose in pitch.

She nodded.

"Then get out!"

Tears rolled down her cheeks as she slowly shook her head, her eyes large and dark, fixed on his face. "Please let me help you, *liebling*. I love you. I will not abandon you. I will not let this Niesner use you against my country. We Israelis will find out the truth. We shall bring this Niesner down and then you shall be free."

He rose to his feet and walked over to her. "Get out."

She looked up at him wordlessly, slowly shaking her head.

He struck her across the face with the back of his hand. "I said, get out."

She got unsteadily to her feet, a hand raised to the cheek he had struck. Her wounded eyes sought his. *"Got vet shtrofen,"* she said in a harsh whisper. "God will punish."

"There is no God," his voice was flat, resigned.

"But there is, my *neshomeleh*. He will punish those who did this to you."

"Get out."

She turned at the door. "I love you."

"Get out!" His voice cracked in a half shriek.

"Shalom," she whispered and left him.

Scott stood staring at the closed door for a moment. Then he turned, a grimace of pain and despair distorting his face, and with shaking hands poured himself another drink.

About ten o'clock he left his apartment and drove his Opel to the Embassy on Boltzmangasse. He parked on the deserted street in front of the building, nodded pleasantly at the guard, and entered through the familiar ornate doors. He took the small elevator to the fourth floor and walked down the deserted hallway to his office.

Turning on the lights he sat for a few minutes perched on the edge of his desk smoking a cigarette. He reached into a desk drawer and took out a small camera with a large lens attached to it. He adjusted it carefully. He then extracted some keys from his pocket and progressively unlocked a complicated series of locks on a door leading to an adjoining room. The room was small and square with one heavily barred window. Two green steel filing cabinets stood against one wall, each locked by a sturdy steel rod extending down their length and secured by a padlock. Scott turned on the overhead light and unlocked one of the cabinets. After a careful examination, he removed a file folder and spread its contents out on the top of a flat table nearby. He turned on a goosenecked lamp with a green metal shade and twisted it until it brightly illuminated, without shadows or glare, one of the pages from the file folder.

He hesitated, paused, wiped his perspiring face and wet palms with a handkerchief and then began carefully to adjust the lens opening and range of the camera. Holding the camera about eighteen inches from the page, he took a picture. In rapid succession he placed each page in the file folder in the same position under the lamp and photographed it. Five minutes later, having left the file room and his office as he found them, he drove off into the night with the roll of exposed film in his pocket.

Brune and Sessena were playing two-handed bridge at midnight in the small paneled library of the house in Heitzing when the telephone rang. They let it ring four times and it then fell silent. Immediately thereafter it rang again. Sessena picked it up on the third ring. "Yes?"

"Can you pick me up at the usual place?" Scott's voice asked.

"Yes. Give us fifteen minutes. Are you clean?"

"I am sure of it."

"Be right with you."

As soon as the car swung into the curbing on the dark street, Scott slid into the back seat, behind Sessena who drove off at once without speaking.

After a block or so he spoke over his shoulder. "O.K., Scottie, down on the floor. When we get near to our spot, I'll ask you to put that black hood over your head. Sorry about these precautions, but the less you know about our arrangements the better for you."

"No strain, Ernie," Scott said slipping down into the cramped space between the rear and front seats. "I've learned about my limitations."

Brune and Sessena looked at Scott expectantly in a

.268.

whitewashed room which was almost identical to the many rooms in which they had met in the past.

Scott looked disheveled and his breath smelled of the scotch he had been drinking, but he was not drunk. He reached into his coat pocket and laid the roll of film on the table near his chair. He looked unsmilingly at his companions. "Do you know what that is?"

"You tell us, Scottie," Sessena said softly.

"That is a film of the contents of a top secret file from my section at the Embassy."

"How did you get it?"

"I photographed it earlier tonight. I was on my way across town to give it to someone, I can't remember who, when I came to my senses."

Brune nodded. "Very good."

"Very good?" Scott echoed in a low, strained voice. "Don't you realize that I was in a time lapse again carrying out Niesner's orders under hypnotism?"

"But you didn't carry them out, Scott. You brought the film here instead. That is of immense importance."

"What about next time?" Scott asked in a haunted voice.

"You'll react the same way," Brune said confidently.

Scott covered his face with his hands and kneaded his forehead with his fingers. "I hope I will. I hope to God I will." He looked up at them with tortured eyes. "You don't know, you can't imagine the hell it is to be unsure."

"I'm sure," Brune said dryly. "Where is that faith in

the integrity of the human personality, of the soul as you call it? If you won't believe me, can't you rely on your faith?"

"Yes. Yes, I must."

Sessena cleared his throat, but his voice still sounded husky. "It worked out just right, Scottie. This was another test. We'll examine that film to see if it contains something we can't let Niesner have, if it doesn't, you still deliver it. If it does, we'll expose a substitute film for you to deliver. This will encourage Niesner in his next move."

"But I don't remember where I was to take it!" Scott protested.

"Take it to Niesner on your next visit as an example of the amnesia that is bothering you." Brune spoke while lighting his pipe. "You overlook one very encouraging thing," he continued. "You not only refused to carry out Niesner's orders in full, but you now remember what you did. It's not a complete mental blackout such as you had when you beat up the woman in Rome."

"No, but I did what Niesner wanted and then snapped out of it at the last moment."

"Exactly."

"But I did what he wanted! I actually filmed secret documents because I was ordered to do so by radio! My God! Can't you see how degrading that is?"

"No, Scott, I can't. You didn't deliver them after

filming. You brought them here. That makes all the difference."

"You're doing very successfully, Scottie, just what we set out to do," Sessena interjected quietly. "We have learned about the enemy's mind bending techniques and you are gaining Niesner's confidence so that we can use you as a counterspy. Those are two hellishly big pluses."

"A counterspy," Scott repeated slowly. "The question is would I be a double agent in spite of myself?"

"We don't think so," Sessena said positively. "And you don't either or you wouldn't be in this."

"No," Scott said slowly, "I wouldn't be in this."

"Have you heard anything of the Israeli woman?" Sessena asked.

Scott spoke somberly, nodding. "Yes. She came to me tonight offering love and forgiveness."

"How did you handle it?"

"I struck her and threw her out."

There was an uncomfortable silence. "That was the only way, Scottie," Sessena said softly. "You can't afford to have a loving woman around at this point, especially one with intelligence connections."

"I know. There's neither love nor forgiveness for me. I don't know which one of my personalities was at work when I struck her. I am beginning to fear that it was the only one I've got."

"Would she have gone if you hadn't struck her?"

"No. Probably not."

.271.

"Then you had to strike her, Scottie. It was the only humane thing to do."

Scott's expression was bitter. "Yes, we must always be humane. I was taught that in school."

.23.

Niesner greeted Scott with a kindly professional interest. "I have not seen you for some days. You have now had an opportunity to live your life without the daily attention of your doctor. I suspect that has been a relief, no?" he smiled.

"I have slept a lot and rested as you suggested."

"What? No love life?" Niesner asked jocularly. "I never suggested that you should be a celibate, you know."

"The woman in Rome I beat up, showed up in Vienna. I sent her away."

Niesner nodded. "I think that was wise, since it was your decision. This woman seems to have an unsettling effect on you. The world is full of women, however. Choose another to whom you react differently."

"I struck her, Doctor. Again. That is unlike me."

"Don't worry about it. It was not gentlemanly, but medically speaking it may have been the best thing you could do. I notice you remember this attack. There was no memory blackout. That is good. Already you are not blocking distasteful things out. That is progress. I am encouraged."

"My memory isn't what it was though, Doctor," Scott gave a little deprecating laugh and took the roll of film from his pocket. "I found this in my pocket the other night. I have the feeling that I was supposed to give it to someone, but I can't remember who. And I can't remember how it got into my pocket. It's a small thing, I know, but in my present mental state it worries me."

Niesner shrugged. "Don't let that worry you, Mr. Scott. That is not amnesia or any other mental condition requiring medical attention. It is absentmindedness. I have that problem myself. Lay the film on the table and I'll ask my receptionist to take it to a photographer for you. When you see the pictures you will no doubt be reminded of to whom you wished to give the film."

Scott laid the film on the table which Niesner indicated.

"Now," Niesner said, "let us examine you for a few minutes." The firm fingers sought Scott's temples.

Sessena answered the telephone in the house in Heitzing after the prescribed sequence of rings. "Yes."

"This is the number two boy," Browne's slightly nasal middle border twang came over the wire. "Number one is in the *Allegemeines Krankenhaus,* apparently an attempted suicide."

"What are his chances?"

"Fifty-fifty. It was an overdose of sleeping pills. He's still unconscious and on the critical list. He turned in early and loaded up, I guess. Fortunately, I had to

clear a dispatch with him at ten o'clock. I went around
to his apartment. When he didn't answer and I heard
his radio and saw the lights on, I broke in. Damn
lucky, it was. The hospital internist says we just got
him in under the wire. They pumped him out, but
there's a lot of the stuff in his bloodstream."

"Keep me informed how it goes. Stay with him
every minute; use the other boys to spell off. They
don't need to know any more than is obvious, but don't
let him out of sight. As soon as he is well enough to
move get him down to the place in the country—sub
rosa and I mean sub rosa. If he gives you any trouble,
use force."

"Yes, sir."

"This is a Mayday type of operation. You understand that?"

"Yes, sir."

"O.K. Thanks. Glad you were on your toes. You
were right to call this number." He slammed down the
receiver and shoving his hands deep into his trouser
pockets stood staring out of the garden window into the
impenetrable darkness.

Scott sat in a lawn chair in the warm afternoon sun
gazing out over the sparkling blue water of Attersee.
The gentle movement of the light air through the trees
nearby and the sound of the insects made him sleepy,
which struck him as peculiar. He had slept fifteen
hours a day on the average since he had been brought

to Attersee three days before. Nevertheless, he still felt physically sluggish and thickheaded.

Sessena dropped into a chair beside him. "Nice view."

"Beautiful."

"How are you feeling?"

"O.K. As soon as I have a little more pep, I'll be ready to move on."

"You know what your trouble was?"

"Sleeping pills."

"You're down as an attempted suicide, Scottie."

"It wasn't attempted suicide."

"I'm glad to hear it. Why did you take so many pills?"

"I didn't take very many. I had been drinking pretty heavily and I took a few to get to sleep. It was the combination that did it."

"You should have thought of that."

"I should have. I didn't."

"The doctors said you had the equivalent of ten doses in your system."

"They're nuts. I would have had to have eaten them like popcorn."

"They say you did."

Scott shrugged and looked out over the water. After a few minutes he spoke without taking his eyes from the distance. "Where do we go from here?"

"Should we finish what we started?"

"We have finished it."

"What do you mean?"

"Niesner informed me on my last visit that I was cured."

"No further appointments?"

"No."

Sessena looked contemplatively out over the lake, then his eyes returned to Scott. "Maybe he feels you're programmed."

Scott met Sessena's eyes defiantly. "Like hell. I'm my own man."

Sessena didn't answer. "We could reassign you to McLean, nonsensitive duties, and await developments," he said after a moment.

Scott moved in his chair irritably. "What am I, a security risk? I agreed to this Charlie McCarthy bit because you damn near ordered me to. It didn't work out. Is my career to be ruined because I did what you asked me to do? Was I just a psychiatric guinea pig for Brune?"

"Cool it, Scottie. I'm not saying you're a security risk. I'm just saying that I don't believe Niesner has given up on you. That's good. We can use you as a counterspy as we planned."

"You're wasting your time. Niesner's finished with me."

"We'll wait it out."

"Why not leave me in Europe where they can get at me?"

"It's a small world. They'll get at you in McLean if they want to and it's more convenient for us."

"You mean you can keep me under closer surveillance."

"Do you want to handle this alone? Are you ready to take the risk? I won't argue with you about the sleeping pills, Scottie. You know whether that was an accident or an attempted suicide. Just ask yourself this, 'Can I handle it alone if the message or impulse comes in the night?'"

Scott stared morosely out over the water. He cleared his throat nervously and chewed on his lower lip. "O.K. I'll do it your way."

"Good boy."

The Man Behind the Desk glanced up as Brune and Sessena entered his office in McLean. "Thank you for making this effort, Professor Brune. Ernie, welcome back." As they seated themselves he jabbed at a piece of paper on his desk with a forefinger. "This is a simple personnel transfer order. It will assign one of our brightest young men with a brilliant record to headquarters on detached duty. Ordinarily, I would have signed it with the morning mail without a second thought. I didn't, because some question arises as to whether or not this loyal, dedicated young man is a security risk. I understand that he is a possible security risk because he voluntarily submitted himself to an experiment in the line of duty. It is the inconclusive results of the experiment that makes him a possible security risk. Right?" The last word cracked out like a bullet in Brune's direction accompanied by a hard, flashing look from the iron-gray eyes.

"You put it very well," Brune said calmly.

"What is your recommendation, Brune?"

"I have no recommendation, sir. I can only sum up the situation as I see it. Then you will have to make your own decision."

"Very well, sum it up."

Brune slowly filled his pipe and lit it. When it was drawing to his satisfaction, he crossed his legs and squinted his eyes up toward the corner of the room as if he were looking for inspiration, oblivious of the impatient stare of The Man Behind the Desk. "The first thing I want to say, gentlemen, is that Mr. Scott has rendered a great service beyond the call of duty. It is too bad that in the nature of things he can't be awarded a medal for it. He deserves it as much as any soldier who storms an enemy strongpoint at the risk of his own life." His eyes traveled in turn to the hard eyes and emotionless faces of his two companions. "However, be that as it may be," he continued hurriedly, "I have learned a great deal from Scott's willing subjection to the mind bending techniques of Doctor Niesner about the status of such experiments in the Soviet Union. They are much more advanced than I had believed possible. Through my contacts with Scott I have had many important lines of inquiry suggested to me.

From a scientific point of view, we are heavily indebted to him." He drew on his pipe. "Now, as to the question of Scott's future reliability as an American intelligence officer," he shifted in his chair, "we are faced with a number of imponderables. To weigh these imponderables, let me first review what we know." He ticked off each point by pressing his thumb in turn against his fingers. "First, Scott has been subjected to frequent hypnosis by Niesner and has been, ah, shall we say, mentally manipulated by Niesner while in the hypnotic state. Second, Scott actually responded to externally directed stimuli which induced a state of hypnosis and caused him to carry out instructions previously given to him under hypnosis. In other words, a previously established mental pattern was reestablished over Scott at will by radio-induced hypnosis."

"Do we know that as a fact?" The Man Behind the Desk asked.

Brune smiled. "He attacked, without provocation, a woman with whom he was in love and has no recollection of it. I deduce that this was done while under hypnosis, but it is not susceptible of proof in the legal sense. However, we all have some knowledge of Scott's original character. It is unlikely he would have acted toward this woman as he did of his own volition."

The Man exchanged a look with Sessena and then returned his searching gaze to Brune. "Go on."

"Third, after treatment by me, Scott responded again to Niesner's radio-induced hypnosis, but broke away at the last moment and did not carry out his instructions."

"You refer to the filming of classified documents?"

"Yes. Fourth, Scott tried to commit suicide. Fifth, having survived suicide he is now more relaxed, possibly, I should say, more passive than he has been through the entire experiment."

"Is that good or bad?"

"Oh, very good, I should say. In my opinion, at about the same stage Scott attempted suicide, Fenwick and Boad committed suicide. Of course, they didn't have my counter therapy to aid them, poor devils."

"What's good about it?"

"Scott survived, don't you see? That makes all of the difference."

"Even I can see that difference," Sessena growled.

Brune gave his quick smile. "Touché. But let me elaborate. This mind bending technique creates a great psychological strain. As I once observed to Sessena during our Roman sabbatical, it can lead to madness or to suicide. At this primitive stage in its development the technique can fail because of mental rejection, much like the risk of physical rejection in the case of a heart transplant. All three of your men were well adjusted and in good health. Madness did not come—so they chose suicide."

"You have no doubt it was suicide, or, in Scott's case, attempted suicide?" The Man asked.

"None whatsoever." Brune was positive. "As I have

.281.

said, Scott survived and now, for the first time, to my knowledge at least, we have a human being who has been subjected to mind bending and who has reconciled himself to the results."

"And what does that mean?"

"It means that if he becomes again the subject of radio-induced hypnosis he will carry out instructions previously given to him under hypnosis or he will refuse to act. In the latter case he will 'break away,' inform you, and be ready to act as a counterspy."

The Man Behind the Desk studied Sessena. "You originated these orders, Ernie. What did you have in mind?"

"I think we have to see this through. If Scott is theirs, we've lost one and he'll have to be given a medical discharge. If he's ours, we'll use him as a counterspy. If Niesner's finished with him, as Scott believes, he should be restored to duty as soon as he is fully rehabilitated."

"What do you think, Professor?" The gray eyes swung about. "Can we bring this ruffled bird right into the nest?"

Brune spread his hands, his lips stretched thin in an attempted smile above the teeth clamped on his pipe stem. "That's a policy decision. Over to you, I'm afraid."

"Is he theirs or ours?"

"It could go either way."

.282.

"You're a scientist, Brune," the voice was cold. "You can do better than that."

"I wish I could, sir, but this is a new field of scientific inquiry. I can't emphasize that enough."

The Man Behind the Desk glowered at Sessena.

"Bring him back," Sessena said. "This is part of the game. We have to play it out."

The eyes of The Man Behind the Desk held Sessena's for a moment, the pen poised above the personnel form. Then the pen lowered and scrawled out his signature.

.24.

Scott sat with Sessena in the cafeteria of the CIA headquarters building drinking a midmorning cup of coffee.

"Are you sticking around town over the weekend?" Sessena asked.

"I thought I'd go up to New York."

"You like that town, don't you?"

Scott shrugged and sipped his coffee. "There's something to do. I've already visited the Lincoln Memorial and Mount Vernon. That about does it for Washington."

"Flying up as usual?"

"I thought I would."

"Tell me, it's been several weeks now. Any messages from outer space?"

"No. That's all over. Like I said, Niesner gave me up as a bad job."

"You look some better. How's the insomnia?"

"I've got it licked. I sleep like a baby these days."

"Do you ever hear from the girl?"

"That's all over too," Scott said somberly. He finished his coffee. "How long are you going to keep me playing Scrabble with non-classified material,

Ernie? It's boring as hell and until I get a new security clearance I'm downgraded."

"We spend a hell of a lot of time here at McLean on routine intelligence compilation. You field operatives have to learn that it isn't 'gung ho' here at headquarters. In the States the FBI has all the fun."

"I don't feel that I'm part of the team, Ernie. I feel like a simple-minded nephew surrounded by kindly uncles."

"It's only been a few weeks. Don't push it."

Scott's sad, tired eyes met his. "We just wait?"

"Sometimes that's all you can do, Scottie."

Scott looked at him enigmatically and shrugged.

The Man Behind the Desk lit his pipe and blew out the kitchen match. "How's Scott doing?"

"He's not happy," Sessena replied, "but he's staying out of trouble."

"You have a tail on him?"

"Night and day."

"Scott tumbled yet?"

"No. We have some of our best gumshoes on it."

"Will he blow if he tumbles?"

"Maybe," Sessena spoke with some exasperation, "but what in hell else can we do in the circumstances?"

"Why does he visit New York so often?"

"Boredom. Washington is dead on the weekends and Scott likes the big town. I see no harm in throwing him that bone. We don't want him to resign. Not yet, anyway."

"What does he do in the big town?"

"Theatre, museums, baseball games, the usual tourist bit. He's even taken the boat and viewed Manhattan's skyline from the water. Once or twice he's dropped in to see the action at Virgie Sinclair's hippie pad in the Village."

"You'll have to fill me in."

"Virgie Sinclair, a medium-sized movie star twenty years ago, a TV personality ten years ago, and a reformed lush today, lost most of her marbles with her looks somewhere on the downswing. She's an authentic kook from the reject pile of the entertainment world but she's a shrewd kook and she spotted early the public's current tendency to glorify kooks. She opened a joint in the Village called *Mother Earth*. The hippies flock to it, more or less for free. They provide the color and diversion for the New York swingers that pay the freight by shelling out to spend a few hours 'making the scene.' Virgie presides over the whole circus dressed like a hippie den mother in a red fright wig. I understand she's laughing all the way to the bank."

The Man Behind the Desk was bemused. "Virgie Sinclair. I remember her. She couldn't act worth a damn, but she had a comedy flair."

"She hasn't lost it. In the new environment she just plays it straight."

"Where do you learn all this stuff, Ernie?"

"The FBI."

"Imagine that." The gray eyes drifted slowly up to the ceiling. "These are patriotic hippies, I take it."

"The FBI claims they're true blue."

"That's reassuring, but let's keep worrying about it. Let's worry about everything that concerns Scott." The gray eyes dropped to Sessena's.

"You're waiting for the other shoe to drop?"

"I sure am, Ernesto mio. I sure am."

Scott stood in the center of the long narrow room that contained and compressed the patrons of *Mother Earth* into the pulsating mass that bestowed upon them the anonymous collective identity they sought. Amplified sound and psychedelic colors washed over him in stale air heavy with cigarette smoke, human sweat, alcohol, and other sweet odors he couldn't identify. In spite of the press of bodies about him and the high-pitched, formless shriek of scores of human voices happily and willfully impaled on electronic vibrations, there was an atmosphere of desperation in the room, a resigned surrender to chaos as a refuge from reality.

A sallow-faced young man with a full, soft brown beard, wearing an insane caricature of a frontiersman's buckskin suit, leaned toward him while keeping his eyes on a movie screen suspended from the ceiling where formless shadows in black and white jerked and fluttered. "I'm the Pagan Lover. It's a swinging Friday night, chum."

Scott did not turn to him. "You're late," he said, staring at the movie screen.

"Traffic was hell."

"I have a tail. Watch it."

Brown beard giggled. "Two hopped up chicks have waylaid him back at the door. We can take all the time we need."

They pushed through the crowd and out a battered rear door opening into a dark alleyway. The Pagan Lover handed him an envelope. "Your tickets are inside with a grand and a half in C notes and a selection of foreign funny money. Happy landings. I'll watch the door until you get clear, chum, just in case."

Scott pocketed the envelope and walked down the alleyway. He emerged into a street filled with a jostling crowd in their late teens and early twenties dressed in dusty, shapeless clothes which might have come from a ragbag or from a theatrical costuming rental agency. He pushed by a pale-faced, hollow-chested group standing aimlessly near the curbing under a streetlight and entered a taxi whose glowing roof sign indicated that it was for hire. "Kennedy Airport. There's an extra five for you if you break out of here fast and make it to Pan American in forty minutes."

The driver pushed down the flag on his meter as he started the motor. "You mind if I run over a few of these creeps?"

"Not much."

The driver moved away from the curbing, honking

his horn and shouting out of his window at both pedestrians and competing automobile traffic. "Once I get out of the Village, we're O.K.," he said over his shoulder. After five minutes of strenuous maneuvering they emerged from the crowded, narrow streets and shortly thereafter dipped into the midtown tunnel leading to Queens. The driver relaxed, and steering with one hand, laid a hairy, beefy arm along the back of the seat inside an aluminum frame containing an open sliding shatterproof window. "It's none of my business, Mac, but just in case you forgot, what about the luggage?"

"It got lost on a connecting flight. They say that they'll send it on."

The beefy arm beat against the seat. "They say. They say. Christ, I just hope you see it again. You got no idea how many people get into this cab and tell me the airlines lost their luggage. You know, they ain't just transporting bodies. A guy needs his clothes unless he's heading for some nudist camp."

Scott, staring with a little frown out of the window, didn't answer.

"Where you headin', Mac?"

"Look, buddy, stop the yak-yak. Let's get to Kennedy. The five bucks is for speed, not conversation."

"O.K. O.K. So you don't want to talk. That I can understand. The wife gives you plenty of that at home, right? I'll give you complete privacy." He slid the window closed and hunched over his steering wheel, a heavy-shouldered figure with a crew haircut, now imperfectly visible through the scratched and milky surface of the glass. Scott gave an involuntary sigh and lit a cigarette as he leaned back against the seat. He threw the burnt match onto the scuffed rubber floor mat where it rested with more passenger debris, cigarette butts, chewing gum wrappers, and other spent matches. He rubbed his eyes and then closed them as he smoked.

He still had not been to bed when the Pan American flight landed at Vienna. He took a taxi to a small, walk-up hotel in the *Innerstadt* and after a shower in the communal bathroom on his floor fell into a deep sleep across a swaybacked bed in the dingy, high-ceilinged room he had engaged. It was dark when he awoke. He washed and shaved with a razor from his coat pocket at a lavatory set in a frame of cracked tile against one wall, dressed again in the wrinkled clothes he had flown in, and stepped out into the street in front of the hotel.

A slight breeze stirred as he strode down the narrow sidewalk toward a lighted main thoroughfare at the foot of a curving slope. A taxi ride took him across the *Innerstadt* to a small tobacco shop. He glanced at the dull metal shutters drawn down and locked over its windows and rang a bell set in the frame of a door opening on a staircase landing leading to an upper story. After several peals of the bell, he heard footsteps descending the staircase. There was a silence followed by the click of a heavy lock. The door opened a few inches, restrained by a length of chain. A short, stocky man with squinting eyes peered out at Scott, breathing asthmatically. *"Ja?"*

Scott handed him a hundred-shilling note with the upper right corner turned down.

"Just a moment." The man unfastened the chain and opened the door. "Up the stairs, *bitte*. The room to the left at the top."

Scott walked up the stairs and entered a small, over-furnished room. It was heavy with the stale smell of cooking and tobacco smoke. The man, breathing hard, entered the room behind him and shut the door. He did not invite Scott to sit down. His eyes, revealed in the lamplight, were a watery blue. They appraised Scott shrewdly. *"Ja?"*

"Herr Oberdorf?"

The man nodded.

"I need new papers, a new passport."

Oberdorf gave a short jerky nod. "You have a passport now?"

"Yes."

"What nationality?"

"American."

"Gut." Oberdorf extended a stubby hand.

Scott hesitated.

"I must have your present passport. It is a part of the price. I shall adapt it for the use of others."

Scott handed it to him.

Oberdorf inspected it very briefly. *"Gut,"* he grunted. *"Zehr gut."* He glanced up at Scott. "What nationality do you wish?"

"Canadian. I'm no good at acting."

"Name?"

"Henry Perry."

"Occupation?"

"Businessman."

"Address?"

"1781 King Street, Vancouver, British Columbia."

"Date and place of birth?"

"Vancouver, August 10, 1940."

"You wish a travel history in it?"

"No. Just bring me here as of yesterday."

Oberdorf took some notes on Scott's appearance. He nodded toward a corner of the room where a camera stood on a tripod between two unlighted flood lamps. "Come over here. I shall take your picture." When he had finished he turned to Scott. "Come back tomorrow night at 2200 hours. It will be ready. It will cost you two thousand American dollars."

"An American passport is worth fifteen thousand dollars on the black market," Scott said. "A Canadian passport is worth less than ten thousand dollars. If you keep my passport you owe me money."

Oberdorf's face slowly broke into a mirthless grin, revealing widely spaced, yellowed teeth. "You forget the element of need, Herr Scott. I am prepared to wait to realize on my investment. You, if I am not mistaken, cannot wait."

"I can't give you more than one thousand dollars. Otherwise, I'll have to take my chances with the American passport."

Oberdorf searched his face for a moment, then he shrugged. "I am naïve, perhaps. I believe you. One thousand dollars at 2200 tomorrow night."

Scott put out his hand. "I'll need my passport until then."

Oberdorf reluctantly handed it back. "So you will." He moved toward the door. "I shall show you out." They descended to the street level. The cool, fresh night air swirled about them on the lower landing as Oberdorf opened the unchained and unbolted door.

"Auf Wiedersehen," he said softly. Scott edged by him and disappeared into a cotton-like mist that had risen from the Danube and was now silently enveloping the city.

He checked out of his hotel before he returned for his new passport and afterward registered under the name of Perry at a similar-type hotel on *Wahringstrasse.* Fifteen minutes later he was staring morosely out on the street from the small worn lobby. He did not feel like sleep. He wanted to walk. He stepped out into *Wahringstrasse,* coatless and hatless, ignoring the light rain which had begun to fall. A dusty Mercedes 250 sedan pulled alongside him at the curb. Lani Evron called to him from an open back window. "Get in, *neshomeleh,* quickly."

He hesitated and then stepped into the automobile. The driver, flanked by a burly fellow in a cloth cap, ground the gears as the car lurched out into the traffic. Scott nodded toward the front seat. "The Rabbi?"

"Yes."

"He should learn how to drive."

She smiled at him affectionately and reaching out, placed a hand over his. "How have you been, *liebling?*"

"Swell."

"I have missed you."

"I've missed myself."

She looked at him searchingly. "Are you all right?"

"Sure."

"You are very thin, and your clothes. . . ."

Scott shrugged.

"Why have you returned to Vienna, Bob? You are not on a CIA assignment."

"Can you be certain?"

"Yes, I can be certain. We have followed every move you've made and we have some contact within the CIA."

"I forgot that I fascinate Israeli intelligence." He fished a cigarette from a crumpled pack and lit it. In the flare of light his face looked taut and strained.

"Are you going to visit Niesner?"

"Yes."

"*Liebling,* you must not do that. You must not."

Scott inhaled his cigarette and remained silent.

"He is on our execution list, *liebling*. You must stand clear. It will soon be over."

Scott had closed his eyes. He now slowly opened them. "Why?"

"We have decided that he is a Russian spy master working with the Arabs. We have decided that he was the control for Fenwick and Boad." She paused. "And for you."

"Me?"

"Yes, *liebling*. I am doing you a favor, you see. Stand clear."

"Niesner is my doctor. Nothing more."

She made an impatient gesture of dismissal. "We know better. We now know that he is a mind bender, a highly scientific destroyer of human will."

"Not in my case."

She looked at him compassionately. "In your case, too."

He grimaced and looked out of the window.

"He will use you against Israel as he did Fenwick and Boad. We can't allow that. You must stand clear. If you do, you are in no danger. We don't want to kill you also, *neshomeleh*. You are not our natural enemy. At most, you are our unnatural enemy."

Scott sighed. "Most unnatural."

She leaned over and kissed him lightly on his thin cheek. "We have circled and are again near your hotel. Stay in it for twenty-four hours and return to America."

He slowly shook his head.

"Please, *liebling*. I tell you this because I love you. If you ever loved me, do what I ask."

His eyes met hers. "No, I can't stand aside."

A look of resignation came over her face. "Very well. We must play it all out like puppets, mustn't we?"

"Yes. We must play it all out."

It was after midnight when he walked past the looming bulk of *Karlskirche* and turned down the street leading to Doctor Niesner's apartment. At Niesner's request, the concierge had left the outer door on the latch before going to bed. Scott ignored the locked and darkened elevator and walked up the curving stone staircase to the fourth floor. Niesner greeted him with a curt nod at the landing and led him silently through the small parlor into the overfurnished salon. He eyed him coldly. "You look disheveled, Scott. You must watch that. You will call attention to yourself."

"I'll remember."

"You have established your new identity?"

"Yes. I am now Henry Perry."

"Not Scott?"

"Not Scott."

"What is your home address?"

"1781 King Street, Vancouver."

"Occupation?"

"Businessman. Poultry farm equipment."

"Why are you in Europe?"

"I am going to Bucharest to sell equipment to the state farms."

"Who will you contact?"

"Gheorghe Ionesco at the Ministry of Agriculture."

Niesner nodded. *"Gut."* His eyes held Scott's. "You will take your further orders from him. Do you understand?"

"Yes."

"He will tell you the circumstances under which you are to visit Jerusalem. You are to follow his instructions to the letter."

"Yes, to the letter."

Niesner turned on a brighter lamp. "Now let me examine you. It has been some weeks. We must take no chances."

Scott moved obediently to the chair Niesner indicated. "There is something I should tell you, doctor."

"Yes?"

"The Israeli intelligence knows about you. You are on their execution list."

Niesner's expression froze. *"Ja?"* How do you know this?"

"They told me."

"They told you?"

"Yes." Scott's lips formed a faint smile and then

.298.

drew down at the corners as he continued to look at Niesner. "You are on my list too."

Niesner stared down uncomprehendingly at the Walther PPK pistol which had appeared in Scott's hand. "Your list?" The words came out flatly.

Scott's voice remained low, but became metallically hard. "It didn't work, Niesner. It didn't quite work. I've broken out of the snare. I'm free."

Niesner wet his lips with an unconscious flick of his tongue and looked deeply into Scott's eyes. "You are confused, Scott. You are talking to your doctor. Put the gun down."

Scott's smile widened and he slowly shook his head. "Not tonight, Josephine."

A look of alarm began to creep across Niesner's face. He cleared his throat. "Put the gun down." He tried to speak authoritatively, but fear was working now and his voice cracked.

Scott's expression became bland. "You are beginning to believe it now, you bloodless son-of-a-bitch," he said almost caressingly.

A bead of perspiration, forming where the thin steel of the frame of his glasses touched the gray hair below his temples, ran down Niesner's cheek. He tried to speak again, but faltered, his lips moving over unuttered words. Scott continued to grin at him in the silence that enveloped them. An ornamental Swiss clock on the mantel behind Niesner swung its bright circular pendulum back and forth briskly. From the street, beyond the heavy drawn draperies and the double windowpanes, came the muted sound of an automobile horn.

Scott waited. Niesner began to tremble, his facial muscles working. His eyes filled with tears behind his glasses. He looked at Scott beseechingly. Still Scott waited. "This will be for all of us," he said at last, emphasizing each word. He squeezed the trigger. The gun's percussion, muffled by its silencer, sounded in the quiet of the room like a cane struck across a tabletop. Niesner spun backward from the impact of the first bullet, staggered as the second bullet struck him, and fell heavily between a sofa and a ladderback chair. Scott stood over him a moment, his face granite hard, then he reached over to the mantel, grasped a blue porcelain vase full of flowers, and emptied its contents over Niesner.

He pocketed the gun and moved quickly and lightly across the heavy carpeting to the apartment door. He opened it carefully, peered into the hallway, and stepped outside, closing it softly behind him. He listened intently for a moment and then ran to the staircase. At the street entrance he drew a deep breath and forced himself to open the heavy door with casual slowness. He crossed the street, threading his way among parked cars, and walked rapidly toward *Ringstrasse*, fighting the sense of exaltation and excitement that was surging through him. He had made it, by God. He had emerged from the end of a long tunnel of nightmares, his own man at last, but he could not let his emotions take over. He had more calls to make.

Lani Evron, standing in the shadows with the two other Israeli agents, watched Scott emerge from the apartment building.

"That's Scott," the Rabbi whispered. "Shall we get him?"

Lani looked after the retreating figure. "No, let him go. It would only complicate matters. We can find him if we want him."

They cautiously entered the apartment building and climbed the stairs to Niesner's floor. Lani walked to the door of the apartment and rang the bell as her companions flattened themselves along the wall on either side. When there was no response, they quickly and deftly forced the lock and entered. They found Niesner on his back, a bloodstain beneath him spreading slowly over the carpet. Lani leaned over him and felt his pulse. "He's still alive, but it's just a flutter."

"Scott?" Cloth Cap asked.

Lani nodded, a happy smile of comprehension spreading across her face. "Yes, that must be it. It was Scott."

The Rabbi looked down at Niesner. "Should I give him the *coup de grâce* for Israel?"

Lani was looking into the distance, a smile still playing about her lips. She became aware of the question and looked down at the crumpled figure on the floor. Her face grew cold. "No, take him with us. We may be able to put him to some use, dead or alive."

Scott passed through London customs and immigration the next morning as Henry Perry. He bought two shirts, two changes of underclothing, and a cheap suitcase at an airport arcade. After shaving, washing, and changing, he boarded an afternoon plane for Montreal with a connection to Chicago. At O'Hare Airport he hailed a taxi and gave the driver the address of a southside hotel near Jackson Park and the Midway campus of the University of Chicago. He dialed the telephone number of the university central switchboard as he sat on the edge of the bed in his room. On the second ring he heard the slurred greeting of a telephone operator.

"I wish to reach Professor Brune in the psychology department, please."

"I'll give you information." There was a sharp pop and a crackle on the line.

"Information." The syllables were spoken as four distinct words.

"Can you tell me where I can reach Professor Brune of the psychology department?"

"I can connect you with his office."

"Please." Scott lit a cigarette, holding the telephone cradled between his shoulder and his cheek.

"Professor Brune's office." The voice was feminine and slightly nasal.

"My name is Henry Perry. I was a student of Professor Brune's a few years back. I am in Chicago between planes and I wonder where I could find him this afternoon or this evening."

"Professor Brune is downtown today, Mr. Perry. Let me see. No, I am afraid that we have no place to reach him. He does have a lecture here on the quadrangles tonight at eight o'clock. Why don't you audit that? Many of his former students do. I know that he will be delighted. He likes to stay in touch."

Scott wrote down the name and room number of the building she gave him and hung up the telephone. He flexed his shoulder muscles and glanced at his wristwatch. There were several hours to wait. He left the hotel and walked southward through Jackson Park to the public beaches of Lake Michigan. The day was overcast with rain threatening and the beach was deserted except for two teen-age boys in swimming shorts and faded blue sweat shirts throwing a leather volleyball back and forth. Scott sat on a stone retaining wall and looked out over the gray lake. The pumping station was silhouetted against a sharp horizon where the leaden sky brightened to a pale yellow over the invisible Michigan shore. A barely perceptible surf lapped at the beach without enough force to reach a sand castle built and abandoned by some now-absent child.

Scott felt his inner tension subside. He decided that he would buy a pair of trunks and go swimming. He would swim out into the lake as he used to do from the

.303.

Indiana shore until he felt that he had gone almost too far. Then he would swim back, using a slow, easy crawl, pacing himself, conserving his strength, testing himself within the limits of his endurance, secure in the self-knowledge which was the bedrock on which his calm, quiet personality had rested. He sensed that self-knowledge slowly returning as on a flood tide. He would swim out into this familiar lake and rediscover more of himself. Then he would go see Heindrich Brune. A little smile of anticipation played about his lips as he rose to go. He picked up the errant volleyball that had rolled under his feet and, grinning, threw it back to the two boys.

The evening class in advanced psychology at The University of Chicago was half over when Scott entered the amphitheater-like room with its soaring gothic windows and sat down in an empty seat behind the last curving file of benches that rose in tiers from the professor's dais. Professor Heindrich Brune was lounging against his desk, his hands thrust deep into his trouser pockets, speaking easily in his distinctive drawl. He gave no indication that he had seen Scott enter the lecture room and affected surprise when Scott rose to meet him as he hurried up the broad steps of the aisle after the lecture was completed. "Why, Scottie, this is great! Auditing my classes, eh?" He tried to edge past. "I have to run. I'm on just one hell of a schedule. Drop in and see me tomorrow. I'll take you to lunch."

Scott continued to block his way as the last student filed past and they were left alone in the empty room. "I'm flying out tonight, Professor. I want to see you now."

"I'm afraid that is quite impossible, Scott. I have prior commitments." He tried unsuccessfully to push by again. He stood back, looking at Scott. "Are you trying to prevent my leaving this room?"

"That's right."

"It's an outrage. You can't do that."

"No?" Scott smiled thinly.

"What's the matter with you, Scott?"

"You might well ask, Professor."

Brune bit his lip nervously. "I've heard from Sessena. They are looking for you."

"You weren't rushing to telephone, by any chance?"

"Of course not," Brune said unconvincingly.

"We are going to where you keep the records on my case," Scott said quietly. "I want to see them."

"I can't do that!" Brune protested.

"Why not?"

"They haven't been fully evaluated. They aren't available for release. In their present form they would be misleading."

Scott's eyes glinted. "I'm sure of that." His expression hardened. "You'll release them to me. I'm the guinea pig, remember?"

"I'll do no such thing."

Scott lifted the pistol in his right hand far enough so that Brune could see it. "I think you will."

"You are threatening me with a pistol in my own classroom?" Brune asked incredulously. "You've gone berserk!"

"Not yet, Professor, but I'm teetering on the edge. I've killed Niesner. I won't much mind killing you."

Brune blanched. "Very well," he said thickly, dropping his eyes. "Follow me."

"No tricks. No signals. This is my kind of game, not yours. One false move and I'll shoot."

Brune nodded, swallowing and clearing his throat nervously.

They walked through the deserted Gothic quadrangles, striding from darkness into the puddles of light thrown by the wrought iron lamp posts and into darkness again, Scott a casual half pace behind Brune, until they reached an unlighted, gray limestone building.

Brune tried the door and turned to Scott. "It's locked. I'm afraid that's it."

"Use your key." Scott's voice was ominous.

Brune hesitated and then took a key ring from his pocket and fitted a key into the door. They walked across a lobby lit by a night light to a stone staircase and climbed to the second floor. Brune unlocked the door to an office and flicked on a light switch as he entered. He turned to Scott who had crowded in behind him and had closed and locked the door. "Really, Scott. You mustn't do this. It's most irregular. I shall have to report it."

"Shut up."

"After all, we are civilized men," Brune's voice trailed off weakly as he saw the expression in Scott's eyes.

"Where are the records?"

Brune looked around the cluttered office, his eyes moving across several scratched green filing cabinets. "I'm not sure."

The back of Scott's free hand struck Brune across the face. "Get sure."

Brune's trembling fingers touched the edge of his mouth where a trickle of blood had appeared. "That was unnecessary," he said in a trembling voice. "You needn't act like an animal."

"No? What should I act like?"

Brune met his eyes and then averted his gaze. "I'm sorry, Scott. I know that you have been through a lot."

Scott's mouth twisted. "You always were the master of understatement, you self-righteous bastard."

Brune continued to avert his eyes. "Are you sure you are quite yourself, Scott?" The voice was subdued. "Do you really want to force me to do something against my will? You are committing assault and battery. You will have to answer for it."

Scott's laugh was a short, hard ejaculation. "Show me the records."

"What do you want of them? They will be incomprehensible to you."

"I am going to destroy them. I am going to wipe the slate clean."

Brune raised his eyes to Scott's. He was aghast. "You can't do that, Scott. All of my work will be lost!"

"Exactly. We're going back to the status quo, Brune. All the way back. I'm flying about the world reassembling my personality. Part of it is in your files. Get it."

"You're insane. One can't destroy scientific data!"

"No?" Scott's voice was a menacing purr. "Only people?"

"I won't cooperate." Brune's voice was edged with hysteria. "It was a mutually agreed-upon experiment. You were a willing volunteer. You are being most unfair, Scott. Most unfair." His voice broke.

Scott struck him a second time, waited a moment and struck again viciously. "I'll do this as often as I have to, Brune," he said in a husky near-whisper. "We have all night if necessary. All night long."

Brune spoke through cracked lips. "They are in the top drawer of file cabinet B."

"Get them out."

Brune went over to the file cabinet, unlocked it, and then spun around, throwing a heavy iron paper hole puncher at Scott's head. It narrowly missed, landing on the floor behind him with a crash. Scott moved rapidly across the room and seized Brune by the lapels of his tweed jacket. He threw him hard against the filing cabinets and slashed twice at his face with both fists. Brune slumped to the floor unconscious. Scott took off the tweed jacket and threw it to one side. He then tore the shirt from Brune's back and ripped it into strips. Taking an ornamental handkerchief from the jacket, he stuffed it into Brune's mouth and gagged him with a strip of shirting. He roughly rolled him over and tied his wrists behind him. He then tied his ankles to his wrists. He lifted the body up and let it fall with a thud behind the desk where it was concealed from the door.

Wrenching open file cabinet B, Scott lifted out several file folders and hurriedly went through them. He walked into a small toilet off the office and dumped the contents of three folders on the floor. Then he began to methodically tear them up and flush them down the toilet.

It was raining lightly when he emerged from the building and turned toward 59th Street. He passed a couple in a wordless, close embrace in the shadows of an archway beside Harper Library and stepped out to the curbside. He waited for a few minutes, partially sheltered from the rain by the heavy foliage of the great trees arching overhead, until a lone taxi came by. It was a pleasant late hour ride to the airport through empty wet streets and over the lightly traveled expressway. He hardly was aware of his bruised and swollen knuckles.

The plane landed at Washington's National Airport just after it reopened in the morning to receive the jet flights banned in the nighttime hours. Scott had his morning shave again in the men's room. He looked critically at his unchanged shirt in the mirror. It appeared surprisingly fresh. No one in the capital's neat, well-dressed world would notice him unless he developed a facial tick or threw his head. Even then it would be assumed that he was an active member of a government think tank worn thin by the effort to rationalize every action or nonaction in an irrational world.

He bought a magazine and waited until he could go to McLean and enter CIA headquarters with the morning shift, the nine-to-five squares that made even intelligence work bureaucratic and dull as they engaged in the endless point and counterpoint of a paperwork world relieved only by the frequent ingestion of stale coffee with or without powdered cream, with or without sugar or a sugar substitute, served in disposable containers that were carefully and ceremonially burned with the rest of the CIA's paper in compliance with security regulations.

The guard inside the CIA headquarters building at McLean glanced casually at Scott's identification card as he walked past. Scott had disappeared into the elevators before the guard's forehead wrinkled and he walked over to his desk to consult a list. Cursing under his breath as he found Scott's name, he hurriedly dialed a telephone number.

Sessena slammed down the telephone and bolted from his office. He ran down the hallway, past red, green, and yellow doors to the blue door of the office of the Man Behind the Desk. "It's decorated these days like a Goddamned bordello," he thought to himself. "Is he in?" he asked perfunctorily of Miss Hare, scarcely pausing in his rush as she nodded.

The Man Behind the Desk looked up wordlessly as he entered.

"Scott's in the building," Sessena said breathlessly. "Some stupid jerk let him by and then it penetrated thirty seconds later. The thirty seconds were enough."

The Man grinned at Sessena's discomfiture. "You didn't expect this, did you, Ernie?"

"No. The last I heard he had left an open trail to Vienna. There he disappeared. Niesner's disappeared too, I'm told by Browne at the post." He glanced at his watch. "It's nine-ten. He came in with the morning crowd. What in hell is he up to?"

"Maybe he's reporting back to work," the voice was dry. "We've kept this very hush-hush, other than trying unsuccessfully to alert the security guard. We may have overdone it. Have you tried his office?"

"No."

"You might do that." He reached for the ringing telephone. As he listened, speaking monosyllables, he held up a restraining hand. His forehead was furrowed as he returned the phone to its cradle. "That was Chicago. Professor Hal Brune was found semiconscious in his office this morning, trussed up like a Christmas turkey. His files had been ransacked. They don't know yet what is missing or who did it."

Sessena's eyes met the gray ones across the desk. He slapped his hand down on the surface. "He's after the records."

"Better hurry."

Sessena turned and plunged out of the office on a dead run.

Scott stepped from the crowded elevator humming a little tune. He walked down the hallway and entered a door. He handed a familiar-looking chit to a male clerk behind a counter. The clerk walked back to a series of file cabinets and returned with a thick folder. "Sign here, please, sir."

Scott scrawled his signature and placing the folder under one arm sauntered away.

Sessena burst into the room ninety seconds later. "Any visitors yet this morning?" he asked curtly.

"Visitors?"

"Sign-outs of files, research permits, within the last few minutes."

"One officer, sir." The clerk looked at his slips. "Mr. Scott, room 530."

"What did he sign out?"

"His personal records, sir. Any officer is entitled to that, sir."

"Weren't these classified, for God's sake?"

"Yes, sir. I noticed that, but they were the officer's own and he had a chit."

"I suppose if I had a chit for it, you'd hand over the Washington monument."

"Well, hardly, sir."

Sessena swore and reached for a telephone on the counter. "Get me the security guard in one God-damned hell of a hurry."

Scott nodded pleasantly to the secretaries in the elevator and still humming walked down the corridor to Sessena's empty office. He opened the door, peered in, and then quickly entered, closing the door behind him.

His eyes moved about the impersonal room. Sessena left no impressions wherever he went. In his absence from this cubicle it was impossible to imagine from its appearance the type of person who ordinarily occupied it. There were no pictures, no personal belongings; even the air had been efficiently withdrawn and replaced through ducts since Sessena had bolted down the hallway.

A battered, metal government-issue wastebasket was in a corner behind the desk. Scott walked over, lifted it up, and placed it in the center of the floor. He opened the file folder and let the paper it contained flutter into the basket. He spun the wheel of his pocket lighter until it flamed and ignited the contents. As the fire rose up he sat down in the room's swivel chair and placed his feet up on the battered desk. He touched the lighter to the end of a cigarette and inhaled deeply. A happy, carefree grin spread across the worn face as he gazed upward at the ceiling and waited for Sessena.